THE
FALSE

CLAIMED BY THE RED HAND 2

SHAMAN

THE

FALSE

CLAIMED BY THE RED HAND 2

SHAMAN

JORDAN CASTILLO PRICE

JCPBOOKS.com

Print edition published in the
United States in 2025 by JCP Books
www.jcpbooks.com

First Print Edition

ISBN-978-1-944779-45-0

Names and Places

NAMES

Archie - slave from Wildwood in the territories
Taruut - late orc shaman
Droko - replacement shaman from Two Swords Clan
Crespash - Droko's goblin slave
Akala - Droko's betrothed
Kof - Shaman Honor Guard Captain
Gorgul - Shaman Honor Guard Lieutenant
Ul-Rott - Red Hand chieftain
Quinn - horseman from The Fortifications
Bess - slave from The Fortifications
Marok - orc general
Silver - traveling merchant

PLACES

Red Hand Clan - Clan of orcs led by Ul-Rott
Two Swords Clan - Droko's defeated clan from across the river
Fortifications - massive walled city surrounded by wild territories
Wasteland - large stretch of barren land beyond the territories

1

DROKO

The Dead Man's Cliff loomed above me. It blotted out the noonday sun. Formidable, to say the least, an absolute brute of a climb. And at the crest, the telltale glint of stormsilver beckoned.

It was high—much higher than it had looked from a distance—and I was no climber. But for even a walnut-sized nugget of the precious metal, it would be worth the risk. My mind was made up. I would go back to the Two Swords Clan with the stormsilver in my grasp...or I wouldn't go back at all.

"Is the Great Droko having second thoughts?"

The lisp of Crespash's taunts slithered like worms in the rain. Never mind my slave's thick goblin accent. With his teeth long ago yanked from his skull, he mutilated the common tongue.

But I understood him perfectly well. I'd been ignoring his jibes for years.

He grinned wide, flashing gums the color of stone. "You don't need to prove yourself, you know. You're the chieftain's son—"

"His *third* son."

"And just by pissing upright, you command the type of respect most young orcs would die for. Why break your neck over a silly bit of metal?"

For all that Crespash annoyed me, his council was usually sound. It was merely a matter of considering his suggestion... then doing the opposite. I planted myself at the foot of the cliff and shielded my eyes from the sun, searching for the telltale reflective glint of the precious alloy.

Crespash, as usual, was no help at all. He parked himself under the shade of a nearby aspen and said, "I, personally, wouldn't dream of going through all this trouble to please a woman I hadn't even met. Not to mention the fact that Farya is promised to you, so it's a done deal."

Maybe so, but promises can be broken. Farya's father had betrothed her to me when I was just a boy—before we lost land to the Red Hand Clan. "If there's stormsilver to be had, I'm not walking away without it." In the wake of my clan's defeat, it was more important than ever to prove myself. I placed my back to the sun and squinted harder.

The goblin followed my gaze. "What makes you think there *is* any stormsilver to be had, anyway? Did your shaman feed you another prognostication about your path to success? Maybe it came to him in a dream, or he discovered it among some dusty scrolls...or he read the omen in the sound of a cow's fart. It's all balderdash. You know the only talent he's really got is telling people what they want to hear."

"You wouldn't dare say that in earshot of his honor guard."

"Did you notice any fanatics in white paint lurking around all the way out here at the bluffs? I certainly didn't."

I grunted. My eldest brother put great stock in our

shaman's pronouncements. Though it had always seemed to me that in retrospect, the prophetic utterances were vague enough to fit anything.

Still, I wasn't about to agree openly with a heretical goblin slave. Even if there was no one else around to hear it.

Crespash took up a stick and idly shoved a bird's nest from the tree. It landed with a muffled thump. He plucked an egg from the clump of straw with his stumpy fingers and broke the contents into his mouth, swallowing the glob whole as he eyed the cliffside. "That's a sheer climb. You could break a leg—or your skull. And for what? You've never even laid eyes on this Farya. For all you know, she's nothing but skin and bones, with the personality of a pot of gruel. I'll bet she snores like a congested dwarf."

The goblin was just baiting me. True, I'd never heard any tales of Farya's beauty, or wit, or strength...but she was a chieftain's daughter. She'd at least be well-fed.

There—up by the dangling tree roots—was that a glint? A cloud passed in front of the sun before I could know for sure.

"Y'know what your problem is?" No doubt Crespash would take great pleasure in telling me. "I think you're in love with love. Oh, any orc would swear on the stars, moon and sky that it's not so—but you've got it in your mind that marriage is all about finding that one true mate. You think your life will only start once you move out from the longhouse and establish a household of your own. Pump out a brood of bouncing, green baby orclets, and finally, for once, you'll be happy. Even though you're at your apex right now, and you'll never be anything more than the third son of a failed chieftain—"

"Hold your tongue!"

"Or what?" He flashed his gray gums. "You'll cut it out?"

"First you claim my birthright earns respect, and now it's the pinnacle of a sorry life. So, which is it?"

"I suppose it's only the rambling of a lowly goblin whose inferior mind surely can't comprehend the intricacies of your advanced orcish ways."

I knew better than to dwell on the slave's words—the only point of the conversation was to provoke me. What rankled was that he wasn't entirely wrong. I was itching to get out of the longhouse. To distinguish myself. To be my own man. Things I could only hope to achieve once I'd married. Until then, I would just be another green face in a sea of unproven orcs, living under someone else's roof and following someone else's orders.

And until the time came when I finally took Farya as my wife, I'd have to make sure her father had no reason to change his mind.

Which meant scaling the cliff.

It was a daunting challenge. The stone walls were steep, craggy, and slippery with moss. The tree roots provided ample handholds, but they unraveled when I hauled at them with too much force, leaving me hanging precariously in mid-air. My arms burned as I climbed, forcing me to move quickly between handholds. Every foothold threatened to crumble beneath my feet as I scaled the cliff.

At times, it felt like I was making very little progress, as if I'd been stuck in the same spot for hours. But just when my arms and legs were about ready to give out, I found my final handhold and heaved myself up onto the crest, then stood atop the cliffside looking down at Crespash.

He gave me a bored salute.

Chest heaving, I took in the valley below—and the sight of my home village, with its trampled smithy, and the only smoke coming from cooking fires—and fell to my knees to claw at the earth with my bleeding fingers in search of a fitting brideprice for Farya.

I scrabbled at the dirt, digging through tree root and clay, unwilling to concede that maybe I was wrong, and maybe the glint I thought I'd seen was nothing more than a trick of the light. My hope faded as the sun rose higher in the sky. But just when it seemed all was lost, my fingers hit upon something hard and metallic.

I gripped the rounded lump tightly and pulled with all my might. It came free with reluctance, as if the greedy earth itself didn't want to part with the metal. It was bigger than I'd hoped—the size of a goose egg, maybe larger. As I worked it loose, the ground beneath me began to crackle with electric discharge, and sparks raced up my arms. It was an eerie feeling—like discovering you've been sleeping on an anthill. But I could feel in my bones that this hunk of metal held a great power. Not a *mystical* power. Merely one that would allow me to fulfill my dreams of marrying Farya and establishing my own household.

I tucked the heavy lump away in my belt pouch, descended from the cliff, and headed toward my village with Crespash trailing along behind me, remarking about how the day-long task would have taken little more than an hour, had his claws not been lopped off at the top knuckle years ago, back when he was first captured pilfering from the clan. Maybe so, were it not just as likely he'd have murdered me in my sleep by now. I didn't argue. I was too eager to get back and clean myself up for Farya's arrival.

As we neared the village, I spotted the colors of Farya's clan among our own guard.

"They're early," Crespash said.

"Maybe it's better this way."

The goblin smirked. "Well, I'll be. Is that a hint of optimism I detect?"

"Only logic. If their chieftain sees what I went through to capture the stormsilver, it will have more impact than if I just presented it to him polished and pretty. He'll see that I'm determined and strong. A fit husband for his daughter."

"Perhaps," Crespash said as we approached the village perimeter. "But I think your elder brother might be more excited about Farya than about the stormsilver."

The visitors had congregated in a place of honor inside our gate, flanked by both their guards and ours as the chieftains conferred. My betrothed was just a few paces away. She was a handsome young woman, sturdy and serious, with curling dark hair, skin the fresh green of spring moss, and heavily worked armor befitting a chieftain's daughter. But by her side, in the spot where I should be...my elder brother stood. Back straight. Chin raised. And plainly pleased with himself.

I stopped in my tracks, searching for some other possible interpretation of what might be happening. But my eyes didn't lie.

Only my mother noticed me standing with my slave at the gate. She uttered something—a diplomatic excuse, no doubt—and strode over to intercept. Though her hair was shot through with gray now and she could no longer heft a double-headed battleaxe, she still commanded great respect. She greeted me not with the ceremonial words the occasion called for, but with a simple jerk of her head, urging me to veer away from the visitors before I was seen.

I followed her to an empty guard tower, and only once we were far from the rest of the orcs did Matra finally speak.

"Droko—" she said with a deep sigh, "you'll be disappointed by what I have to tell you, but sometimes victory means swallowing your pride. Right now, we're weakened–and we need to keep Farya's father happy. He wants your brother as her husband, so that's exactly what he'll get."

"But she was *promised* to me—"

"And now she's promised to your brother." Matra cupped my jaw and thumbed some grit from my cheek. "Listen, my Little Fearless One." I was glad there was no one else in earshot as she called me by her pet name. And then I heard Crespash snort. "It took a lot of coaxing for them to accept the *second* son of the Two Swords Clan, let alone the third. If your eldest brother wasn't already wed with children of his own, they would have demanded him."

A month ago, our neighbors wouldn't have dared. They were a small clan, and their hunting grounds were poor. Hardly anyone who could make demands. But that was before the Red Hand pounded through our village like a great fist.

Matra went on. "Even with the alliance of Farya's clan, we're still on shaky ground. But there is a way to settle the differences between us and the Red Hand and ensure that if the trolls come clawing at our gates or the ogres raid our stores, the clans will stand together once more, like they did when I was young."

I was disappointed. But I listened dutifully to my mother as she explained how to help my clan...and not on the battlefield with my two best swords. "The Red Hand has extended a treaty—a generous one—that reinstates all our original boundaries to where they were before that cursed river started shifting."

"That *is* generous," I murmured.

Crespash chimed in. "What's the catch?"

"Their ancient shaman is finally dead and they need to replace him. The old man was solitary and he had no followers, so we must surrender our shaman's chief acolyte."

A shaman that was willing to pass on his ways collected followers like a ripe corpse collects flies. I'd never had much use for these so-called mystics. They're sorry fighters, useless at following orders, and insufferable in their attitude toward the rest of the clan. A drain on the clan's resources all around, though occasionally—rarely—an acolyte reveals some ability of his own.

If you believe in that sort of thing.

"What's the holdup?" I asked. "Our temple is overcrowded as it is. Send over the shaman pup and get our lands back."

Matra shook her head in disgust. "If it were that easy, it would be done. But the acolyte was among the first to fall in the Red Hand's attack."

"Then send another. There's plenty to choose from."

"Not one of them fits his description. None of them are Two Swords orcs by birth, as he was. None of them have the same out-curved tusks, or the same flecks of gold in the eye."

"Would it really be so hard for anyone to claim he was a shaman?" Crespash wondered aloud. "Especially if they're destined for a clan who's mostly ignorant of their inscrutable ways."

The goblin was onto something. I said, "There must be at least a dozen other men of the acolyte's age who'd jump at the chance to take the dead orc's place and be known as the one who made Two Swords strong again."

"Oh, there are, my Fearless One. But if this deception were found out, the Red Hand clan wouldn't just reclaim our lands...they'd crush us. And your father can't trust any of those men as well as he trusts you."

I've faced many things in my life with courage. A charging boar. An enemy's blade. Even a raging ogre. But the prospect of marching into a warring clan and declaring myself a shaman filled my belly with unspeakable dread.

My mother thrust a bundle of hides into my hands. I shook it out and revealed a deerskin cloak adorned with cryptic markings and bright feathers. My dread redoubled. She said, "These are your father's wishes. It's your duty to do as he commands."

"It's either that or stand around watching your brother marry your betrothed," Crespash added cheerfully. "Hardly much of a choice, now...is it?"

2

ARCHIE

I've always considered myself a likable guy...but I guess some folks wouldn't agree. There was the brothel owner who tore me from my mother's side in the summer of my eighth year and forced me to go out and beg, claiming I distracted her from her duties. And the stupid boy with the ruddy birthmark on his cheek who pinched me hard enough to leave a welt whenever I got within arm's reach. And the cobbler who'd claimed I stole from his shop, with me clearly barefoot. (When I then praised the comfort of his invisible shoes, it only made matters worse. Go figure.)

None of these tormentors were as big and scary as Taruut's shamanic honor guard. Orcs might be uncharted territory for me...but once you learn to recognize that glint of hatred in someone's eye, it's kind of hard to miss.

The meanest guard was a musclebound crag of an orc named Gorgul, not just any honor guard, but the second in command. Hated me from the moment he laid his beady little eyes on me—and I hadn't even let on how much of a struggle it was to keep myself from calling him "Gargle" by mistake.

The shaman's caves had been my home ever since the orcs sprang me from the slaver's tent. Maybe I was barely conscious for most of the time. But lately, they'd become as familiar to me as anywhere else I've had the misfortune to end up.

The lightless tunnels were confusing at first, but eventually, I learned the twists and turns. Though the air smelled like snuffed candles and the walls were damp, there was a warmth down in those tunnels that had seeped into my bones, which finally let my shoulders unhitch and my muscles relax.

Keeping out of Gargle's way, though–that was the trick. Because without Taruut to remind everyone that my coming was foretold and blah, blah, blah, my burly buddy in the white face paint would just as soon cave in my skull as look at me.

It's easy enough to avoid someone when they want nothing to do with you. But it's not so simple once they're on your tail.

"I know you're here, little human," the orc called out with mock familiarity. Then he made it especially creepy by adding, "I can smell your balls."

Naturally, I did what any sensible person would do: I looked for a place to hide. Sneaking between some arcane orcish shaman stuff in a small chamber somewhere off the beaten path, I prayed to any god who might listen that Gargle was exaggerating. About the balls, I mean.

I've had a noseful of ripe scrotum in my time. More than once. So believe me when I say, with all the mineral baths I'd soaked up since I'd been there, my taint was fresh as a daisy.

But orcs prey on fear, and they'll do whatever it takes to antagonize you. Now, the smell of fear? I had no doubt that stink was something they were intimately acquainted with. So I eased my way between the weird carved totems and the piles of discarded bones, and I willed the big bully of a guard to go pick on someone his own size.

Unfortunately, at that particular moment, Gargle's heart was set on me.

My lantern was shuttered with only a narrow beam leading the way. I had no idea how far the caves extended and could only hope they didn't go on forever. When Taruut died, offerings of food piled up at the mouth of the caves, and I'd managed to nick a few choice goodies. But the offerings were sure to dry up soon.

"If you know what's good for you," Gargle called out, "you'll show yourself...before you really piss me off."

Tough words. But, to my great relief, they were growing distant. The rumble of Gargle's voice echoed off the rocky walls, gradually diminishing until, eventually, it was swallowed by the darkness of the winding caves.

Maybe I couldn't hide forever. But with any luck, I could hold out until Gargle wrote me off as a lost cause and moved on to bother someone else.

I took a pause to scan the chamber I'd fled to—and then I began scavenging for potential weapons. It was a challenge to see by nothing more than my thin beam of light, but I managed. Stalagmites protruded from the floor. Could I break off a chunk and use it as a blade? Only if I had the tools to do so. Which I didn't. Nor the skill, for that matter.

A pile of ancient bones could yield a makeshift club... though that tactic hadn't panned out back when we were first captured and Quinn took a bone to one of our new masters, so I had little hope it would be much help now.

My best bet would be a simple rock. But only if my aim was true.

Plus, why is it there's never a good rock around when you need one?

Just as I was about to give up and admit defeat, my meager light fell on a hefty round stone tucked into the back corner of the chamber. There it was—the weapon I'd been looking for!

But no sooner had I reached for it than the wall I was facing lit up bright, with my own shadow cast in front of me... and a much larger shadow looming up from behind.

Reflexively, I rolled myself into a ball. Not only to make myself a smaller target, but to protect my head. 'Cause I was about to be pounded with something a hell of a lot worse than a rock.

Footfalls scraped against the grit of the cavern floor, eerily soft. No doubt Gorgul's tongue was eager to gloat. He was just making sure he was close enough to enjoy the full impact of his words.

I steeled myself against the fate that had been dogging me ever since Taruut, my protector, drew his last rattling breath... only to be baffled by the very human, very exasperated, very *female* voice that said, "What're you playing at, Archie? It's not as if there's more than one way out of these caves, and you've gotta come out sometime."

The sound registered first, and then it took my eyes a good, long moment to catch up. And not just because of the bright lantern light dazzling my vision. It was Bess, the meek and tearful girl I'd been chained to on my journey to the orc village.

But the woman standing before me now was anything but

meek. And there was nary a tear to be wiped away.

"If you just did what the orcs said, things would be a whole lot easier."

Bess stood with one hand on her hip and the other holding her lantern high—and she was dressed like an orc. I'd only ever seen her in rags, looking frail and battered. But now she was decked out in leather and fur. Her hair was a glossy mop that curled around her ears, and there was a determined set to her jaw. And while she wasn't exactly armed, per se, there was a small eating knife strapped to her belt. She might not be able to fend off a marauding horde with the tiny thing...but it was a better weapon than the rock that just fell from my stupefied grasp.

My old traveling companion was the picture of success... aside from the symbol branded into her cheek. A trio of crossed spears.

I pitched my voice low and said, "Listen. You've got a knife. I'm sure there'll be some kind of ceremonial blade around here somewhere—"

"Don't be dumb. Quinn is fitter than either of us. If he couldn't take down an orc, what makes you think we would stand half a chance? It sounds as if they need you. And for someone like you or me? Making yourself useful is the best way to stay alive. Besides," she gestured vaguely to the world at large. "What's out there for you, anyway? I saw when the guards dragged you into the slaver's tent, after they passed you all around. But me? No one's touched me since I got here. That's more than you can say for the Wasteland."

I searched for some flippant remark to deny it...but that night had been brutal. I'd seen boys die from less.

Then again, I'd almost succumbed to a *cough*. So what did I know?

"I wouldn't be so quick to trust the orcs," I said. "There's one in particular who's got his eye on me. And not cause he thinks I'm pretty."

"Then play up your bond with the shaman."

"Haven't you noticed? The shaman is dead."

Bess narrowed her eyes, but didn't dignify that remark with a response. "I heard the orcs say that an aging shaman should have his replacement trained and ready to go—but Taruut always said the time wasn't right. And it's not like anyone dared contradict him. Even if he was old as dirt."

"Seems kinda morbid to train your own replacement."

"Well, who else is supposed to do your funeral rites? They say another shaman is on his way. Show the new orc how useful you are and he'll keep you around. And anyway, it's not as if you'll get too far outside wearing *that*."

The ragged clothes I'd been given in the slave tent were bad enough. Who knows what became of them? As I convalesced, they'd been swapped out for a slip of cloth around my hips that was little more than a scrap.

Despite the sorry state of my person—or perhaps because of it—I straightened my back and squared my shoulders. "All right," I said. "Let's do this. We'll tell the orcs that Taruut has been using me as an assistant these past months, and I'm the best one to help the new guy settle in."

Confidence is the whole secret behind selling yourself as something you're not. State your case boldly, maintain eye contact, and never back down. I truly had spent plenty of time with Taruut, so I knew how the old man thought. I could do this. I could. And so I abandoned the rock, which frankly wasn't much of a weapon anyhow, and followed Bess out into the cavern where the Honor Guard readied itself for the new shaman's arrival.

Stepping into the light, I announced, "As you all know, Taruut has been acquainting me with the ways of the shaman—"

My posture was proud and my voice was sure, and my statement held the ring of truth. All in all, a promising start.

Though that didn't do me much good when a bored orcish guard shoved Bess aside, whacked me to the ground with the butt of his spear, threw me in irons...and dragged me away.

3

DROKO

I set out for the Red Hand Clan without so much as a word from my father. He was too busy smoothing out his new alliance with Farya's clan to worry about a third son he'd likely never see again. My mother gave me several things: a feather from the shaft of her old battleaxe, a bit of carved horn from the buck I'd felled on my first hunt, and some final words of encouragement.

"Remember, my Little Fearless One...not so little anymore. You serve your clan. And there can be no higher purpose."

It was her blessing to do whatever was necessary, even if it meant I had to sacrifice myself to protect my clan. This was more than just a mission for me—it was my undoing and chance at redemption all at once.

I left without fanfare or adulation—as seemed fitting for the third son of the Two Swords Clan. I left my swords behind, since no shaman would need cold steel when he had his visions to guide him. And I left my proud armor behind as well, wearing only my practice leathers. Because what fool would dare strike a shaman?

But most of all, I left all my hopes and dreams behind. My brother had made off with not only my new home and my betrothed...but the life that should have belonged to me.

The trail between the territories of Two Swords and Red Hand was trampled flat by the tread of scores of soldiers, and one very large horse. A week ago, the road was filled with enemies and the dirt was soaked in brown orcish blood. But now, not even a scavenging raccoon lingered.

"Look at it this way," Crespash said. "You weren't satisfied as third son. The position of Shaman is a big step up for you."

That didn't make me feel any better. A shaman was not only the spiritual leader of the clan, but the advisor to the chieftain. Definitely a higher status than I'd ever aspired to. The only problem?

I didn't have a prophetic bone in my body.

"Here's a thought," Crespash said. "Why don't you try crapping out a prophecy? It's not like shamans really have any special powers. They're just convincing liars."

"That's heresy," I said.

"Among orcs? Maybe. But in case you haven't noticed, I'm not an orc. All I know is, you'd better have your story down by the time we get to the Red Hand Clan. The purported honor of Two Swords depends on it. They'll decapitate you where you stand if they figure out you're a fake."

True enough.

"There is darkness coming," I intoned in my most serious voice. "It will cause trouble for the clan. A problem—a big one. So...we should keep an eye out for it."

Crespash stared at me for a long beat, then said, "That's got to be the worst prophecy I've ever heard. Listen to me, third son. Here's how it's done."

The goblin drew himself up, squared his shoulders, cleared his throat, and lisped, "The wind shall whisper tales of forgotten places and times, and the creatures of the dark shall stir from their slumber. Beware the coming of the full moon, for it will bring a reckoning to test the mettle of even the stoutest warrior."

"What reckoning?"

"Huh?"

"What reckoning?" I repeated. "Is it another clan? Or dissent from within? Or maybe some ogres have decided to—"

"It doesn't matter. It's not as if anyone would dare question the shaman."

I considered his words. "The chieftain might."

"Then claim that the mists of fate have hidden that part of the prophecy from you and shuffle off to consult with the ancestors." Crespash yanked a pouch of dried apples from my belt, tipped the contents into his gummy mouth, then scooped up a handful of pebbles and dumped them into the empty bag. Once he'd swallowed the apples—and it took him several tries—he said, "Everything shamans do is shrouded in secrecy. Lucky for you."

Lucky. Sure. I'd never get to wade through the battlefield with a sword in each hand.

He rehung the bag from my belt and gave it a heft. The pebbles clattered inside. "Granted, you'd be better off if your own venerated spiritual leader had given you a pointer or two. But if the Red Hand shaman took no acolytes, trained no one in his arts…who among them can say exactly what a shaman does or doesn't do?"

Maybe all of this was true. But since when had Crespash

ever tried to steer me right? "If you're hoping to make a fool out of me—"

"I might be an asshole, but I'm not an idiot. If they find you out, what would become of me?"

He had a point.

There was still a long trek ahead of us. As we trudged through the muddy forest, the slave began to collect pieces that could be part of my shaman's paraphernalia. Anything that looked like it could be vaguely mystical was fair game. Overhanging branches, upturned stones, rotting strips of wood—you name it, Crespash stuffed it in our packs.

By the time we approached the eastern gate of the Red Hand Clan's village, my belt pouches were heavy and my satchel was laden with fluff, oddly-shaped rocks, an assortment of leaves and flowers, and innumerable random bones.

He even found an impressive tree branch, filled with gnarls and whorls, which he tied with feathers to create a staff—since, according to him, every great shaman must need a staff.

It was no sword. But it was better than nothing.

Soon the village loomed ahead of us, and I felt my confidence waver. Crespash sized up the pair of guards at the gate. Voice low, he said, "Just remember. They're expecting an adept of your height and your age, with the same flecky eye coloration and the same out-turned tusks. There's absolutely no reason for them to think you're anyone other than who you say you are. Act cryptic and you'll do just fine."

I knew things were bad when Crespash offered a word of actual encouragement.

I might be no shaman, but my station as a chieftain's son served me well. I approached the sentries with my head high, not giving the guards any reason for suspicion. I gave no sign of the relief that flooded me when the guards reflexively took a knee as they pounded their chests and said, "Praise Ul-Rott."

The chieftain's name might be different, but my reply was as reflexive as blinking grit from my eye. My hand fell to the hilt of my blade as I said, "My s—"

Had I really almost answered, *My swords are his?*

I was supposed to be a shaman, not a warrior.

And my hand rested not on a sword, but the hunk of gnarled wood we'd scavenged from the woods.

"My staff," I managed, "is his, for the glory of the Red Hand."

The guards rose, but didn't open the gate. Not until a big orc with honor guard markings painted on his cheeks in white clay shoved through from the other side and demanded of the sentries, "You would keep the new shaman waiting? You're lucky he hasn't cursed you already."

The guards' postures grew a lot more deferential...though I was under no illusion that the one they bore any respect for was me.

The honor guard did not just fold to a single knee. He knelt fully, bending forward until his tusks brushed the ground. A posture of total subservience. "I am unworthy of your blessing." He canted his head slightly and asked, "Erm... your name?"

"Droko."

"Droko the Sage," he finished loudly. Crespash had the good sense not to snort. "I am Gorgul, second in command of the honor guard. And it is my great privilege to serve you."

Gorgul rose and quickly summoned a few of his lieutenants

to march us through the village. Red Hand orcs stopped in the center of the walkways and bowed their heads, making room on the cobblestone paths for us to pass. I was aware that more than one pair of eyes regarded me with curiosity, but thankfully, nobody accused me of being a fraud.

Yet.

The Red Hand village was situated at the foot of a stony bluff, and it was toward this natural wall that Gorgul led us. I expected a dwelling. There was none. Back home, the shaman of the Two Swords clan lived in a grand stilted lodge. It was decorated with signs of his rank, perfumed with incense and the smell of exotic herbs and spices, and surrounded by all of his acolytes and slaves–while the shaman of the Red Hand clan apparently lived in...a cave.

The entrance was hung with a curtain of bones–scores of the tiny things, small and off-white in color, some chalky and brittle, some smooth and shiny. Fingerbones, most likely. And there was no telling what we might find beyond them.

I paused at the curtain, wishing I'd spent more time in the shaman's lodge. Or, frankly, any time at all. At least then I would have some idea what to expect.

Gorgul paused too. He and Crespash and I all stood there looking at each other...and I wondered if my ruse would be uncovered by something as minor as my ignorance about how a shaman should walk through the door.

I steeled myself to be called out...and humiliated...and run through with a vicious, obsidian-tipped spear. But instead, Gorgul averted his eyes and said, "Forgive me, Droko the Sage. Taruut the Wise was a powerful shaman—but he was too old to walk. We carried him everywhere—so we have no order in place for a shaman who can use his own two feet.

Who should lead the way? Command it, and it will be so."

"You know the way," I said. "Proceed." The word even held the ring of authority.

I supposed being the third son of the chieftain was at least good for that.

Bones clattered as Gorgul pushed the curtain aside and led me into the dimness of the cave. I'd expected it to be cool. But the air inside was warm and damp, and the smell of sulfur blotted out every other scent.

The slender cave mouth soon opened into a wide, low chamber. Our guide picked up a lantern and shone it at the far wall. It was covered in carved niches that glinted with crystals, powders, jars of strange liquids, and bundles of herbs and feathers.

Back in the longhouse, despite my parentage, I'd only been allowed to keep what would fit in my footlocker. Clothing and weapons. A whetstone and some coin. And a few precious books from the library my father never bothered to visit.

Here, though, the walls were lined with trinkets and tools. Not one of them familiar.

Thankfully, nobody stopped me on the spot and tested me on the items' arcane uses. Gorgul led us past the carved niches and farther into the caves. His sandals slapped the stony floor as he strode forth like the soldier he was. When he spoke to point out the various hallways, the caves picked up his voice and amplified it, so it seemed to come from everywhere at once.

The passageway branched, and branched again. A labyrinth. And now that we were past the entrance, it looked as though the work had been done not by mallet and chisel, but by nature. The walls were smooth and glistening, striped with different shades of dun and gray. The ceiling undulated overhead, sometimes low enough to make out the pointed daggers of rock aiming down at us, sometimes too high to see at all.

He paused before an archway etched with cryptic symbols in chalky white and brown blood. "These were the personal chambers of Taruut. We only entered to help him into his chair. And even then, we kept our eyes averted. They are yours now."

It was dark, but still I could make out shelves full of more useless junk—jars of mysterious powders and liquids, and strange symbols hewn from bone and stone. A carved sedan chair was pushed against one wall. A sleeping pallet was cut into another, padded with hides.

An old man's room.

I tried to imagine growing so old as to need such things. I had always presumed I would fall in battle. Most likely against this very clan. As I grappled with the bizarre turn my circumstances had taken, a scent teased at the back of my tongue. Beneath the sulfur, the air was thick with an unpleasant odor—a combination of resins, herbs, and smoke. I'd noticed that right away. But there was something else. Something darker....

"It was a few days before we realized Taruut was not just meditating," Gorgul admitted.

Of course. The smell of death.

Gorgul seemed as eager to leave this chamber as I was. He turned smartly and led the way down another branch. "Heated waters run beneath the caves." He showed us into a cavern where a brazier burned low, barely enough to see by.

Smoke gathered at the ceiling. A bowl-shaped depression filled with water took up most of the room. "A few times a day, the Great Whale spouts. Never the same hour...but Taruut the Wise could sense the tremors of the Whale and know when the eruption was coming."

The stone floor was slick and wet, and moisture dripped from the stalactites.

"The Whale spouted just before you got here," Gorgul said. "It will be some time before she spouts again."

The guard led me through various chambers, far more than I would have expected to find beyond the bony curtain that covered the fissure in the rocky cliff face. All of them were filled with dubious trinkets. Most of them smelled of disuse. There were such great stretches of twisting passage-way, so many offshoots and nooks, that eventually they all blended together...until we came upon the archway leading to the shaman's private rooms again.

I was eager to be rid of my guide, but instead of saluting me and heading off to do whatever he normally did, he cleared his throat and said, "No doubt you're wondering why I neglected something so important in your tour."

What was he going on about now? "You tell me."

"The crypt."

"The crypt," I repeated, in the tone my father used when he wanted to watch an opponent squirm.

It apparently worked. Gorgul shifted his grip on his spear—telltale nerves—and said, "Taruut kept its location secret, so we haven't been able to...." He winced.

"Your shaman hasn't been laid to rest?" I demanded, shocked.

"There was no one here to perform the rites."

I wasn't sure which part was worse. That the old shaman hadn't been given to the pyre like a proper orc, or that I was now expected to see him off.

Gorgul said, "Taruut's body lies in state in the village square. The honor of sending him on his next journey is yours."

Spewing a prophecy, I could handle. But the funeral rites of an honored shaman would give away my utter lack of shamanic skills in no time. "Surely the honor should fall to someone from his own clan."

"You are Red Hand now," Gorgul said firmly. "But of course, no one would expect you to prepare the body yourself. If your goblin is not up to the task, you have Taruut's slave at your disposal." That might work. If I got something wrong, I could always blame the slave. "Do you wish to see him?"

I made an impatient gesture, and Gorgul led me deeper into one of the innumerable tunnels we'd toured before. Lantern high, he passed a pair of guards and pushed through a stout iron gate. It was the first chamber we had encountered that was not filled with superstitious nonsense. The room was nearly empty, in fact....

Other than the practically naked human male shackled to the far wall.

My eyes went immediately to the sweep of his pale belly, bared for all to see. Utterly vulnerable. I blinked and looked away, but the sight of the tender, smooth flesh had seared itself into my mind, and I was unprepared for the strength of my reaction. In a deliberately bland voice, I asked, "What is he being punished for?"

Gorgul seemed surprised. "This is no punishment. He's just a slippery one, is all."

Slippery? A cascade of images came to me, unbidden. That smooth, pale belly, oiled and pliant. The sweep of his thigh. The fragile throat that was currently hidden by the tall collar....

Surely a *shaman* wouldn't have such thoughts.

I'd need to watch myself.

Projecting as much boredom as I could manage, I said, "Those neck irons seem like overkill. Get rid of them."

"As you wish, Droko the Sage." Gorgul gestured toward the other guardsmen and they immediately set to work removing the bonds. "You are the shaman."

4

ARCHIE

Obviously, I'd known Taruut's replacement was coming. But what I didn't expect was for him to be a big, strapping specimen of man-meat. Droko the Sage stood tall and strong—easily as tall as Gargle—with shoulders so wide they filled the doorway and hands big enough to circle my waist with ease.

And you know what they say about big hands.

My experience with orcs was fairly limited, but I do know one thing—and that's men. When a man comes sniffing around the red lantern, I can tell which ones would just as soon show me the back of their hand as flash me their dick. I can tell who wants me to simper and preen and play the innocent, and who's hoping I slide a finger up their chute while I suck them dry. But most of all, I can tell which ones really want me.

Given how the young shaman froze the moment our eyes locked, nostrils flaring....

Maybe I could finagle a way out of these chains after all.

Taruut had told me lots of things during our weeks together—but the topic of conversation never turned to sex. It never occurred to me to ask whether orcish shamans were expected to be celibate, like the clerics who rode with the Blood Nomads. Or if they were presented with virgins to ceremonially deflower, like the brutal priests of the Wastelands.

I supposed I was about to find out.

I slumped back against the cave wall as the irons were pried off my neck, drawing the first good breath I'd been able to manage in ages, as I considered just how much flirtation I could get away with. "It will be my pleasure to serve you, Droko the Sage." Orcs get a big charge out of it when you use their name. I knelt, more or less, as much as my manacles would allow. "And I suspect you will find me very...useful."

I let my eyes linger on the new shaman for a fraction of a heartbeat before I cast my gaze downward in a deliberate display of respect. Though before I did, I noted the shaman's nostrils flared again.

Just goes to show, I thought, that deep down inside, men are more alike than different. Even the green, tusky ones. I straightened and put my weight on one leg, canting my hip, displaying my assets to their best advantage.

"Unchain him," Droko said simply, and his guards set to work freeing my hands.

Gargle stepped forward, clearly disapproving. "Archie belongs in the workroom, not roaming through your chambers. In fact, once you're through with him, he should go right to the slave pit."

I had no intention of ending up in a slave pit. Not when a whole different kind of servitude awaited me. But Droko had other plans.

"Archie is to remain with me," he said firmly, his gaze bored deep into my eyes, as if searching for some sort of kinship. I like sex well enough...but after so many years of turning tricks, it's a rare treat to anticipate getting down and dirty with someone.

Had I really ever dreaded getting orced? Silly me. Now I was actually looking forward to it.

And then the shaman hit me with a cold, hard slap of reality when he added, "The human is of no use locked up in here if he is to help me prepare Taruut's body. And give him something to wear. There's frost on the ground."

I'd thought we had a thing between us, Droko and me, but he turned from my holding cell and strode off without a backward glance.

One of the guards tossed me a woolen cloak, so long it dragged on the ground. I headed out of the cave behind Droko, flanked by his guards...including Gargle, of course, who made it very clear by the glares he was leveling at me that he'd just as soon toss me in some pit.

My eyes were sensitive from my weeks in the cave. It was overcast, but I squinted against the haze anyway as we walked the path to the village square. I stole a curious glance at the goblin marching along beside Droko. He was about my height and gangly, with a short body and arms as long as his legs. The last time I'd seen a goblin, he'd been attacking us by the flickering light of a campfire. This one clearly wasn't about to attack anyone. Not only did he have a slave brand on his cheek, but his fingers ended in squat stumps where his claws used to be.

Judging by the scar tissue, the wounds were hardly fresh. In fact, I'd wager they were years old. The finger-stumps were sound and the slave brand was half-buried in the crease at the side of his mouth. He had on a worn shirt and trousers, both of which had seen better days. The fabric was frayed in places and patched up with scraps of cloth in others. But as far as I could tell, he wasn't mistreated.

I'm familiar with the way a bedboy will move, a bit too careful and measured, to act like he hasn't just taken a beating. I've moved that way plenty of times myself. No doubt the goblin had been beaten at some point. But not in recent history.

Even though we were of similar height, his stride was sinuous and strange. He'd be quick, that one—if he weren't shuffling his feet, pretending to be slow.

I hadn't seen much of the orc village when I arrived, seeing as how I'd been carried in, half delirious and wracked with fever. Now, I finally got a good look at the place. First impression?

Neat.

Not in a cobblestones-after-the-rain way, either. Like... freakishly neat.

I'd come of age at the fringes of the Wastelands, in a sizable outpost called Wildwood. The men passing through the brothel were always sure to make some stupid pun about the name as they whipped out their stiffies...and, yes, I would laugh as if they were clever, in hopes of a generous tip. Doubtlessly, there were some parts of Wildwood that were as clean and austere as this orcish settlement—just not any of the ones I'd ever frequented.

Where I came from—the Red Lantern District—the narrow, winding streets were littered with trash. Buildings leaned on each other, their planks weathered and worn. The air carried the smell of smoke and cheap perfume, and the sounds of music and rough laughter echoed through the night—as well as the grunts and groans of paying men determined to get their money's worth.

The only grunts here came from a creature dragging a sledge of lumber down the street–a two-legged giant of a bald, fleshy, gray-green man even bigger than the orcs, wearing nothing but a loincloth and a slave brand.

"What's wrong, little boy?" the goblin chuckled. "You've never seen an ogre before?" He lisped out the word "seen" on a spray of spittle. *No teeth.* "Stupid humans."

It might be my first ogre, but I was a quick learner. I didn't gawk like a tourist. But I definitely kept my eyes and ears open.

Though it was kind of hard to miss the slave pit, where a half-dozen unfortunate souls squatted uneasily in the meager shelter of a sheer wall looking leathery, cold, and utterly miserable.

We made our way farther into the settlement, and soon we reached the village square. In its center was a wooden platform containing just one thing, a simple bier. And on that plain dais was a body draped in cloth.

As I was stewing in my cell these last few days, I hadn't thought much about the old orc who'd been my only companion during my wretched illness. But the sight of Taruut in a funeral shroud made my breath hitch, and I worked hard to swallow past a lump in my throat.

But then another figure joined the old shaman on the bier. And this one was very much alive.

To say he looked formidable would be an understatement. He wasn't the tallest orc around, and a lot of his muscle had gone to fat. But he was decked out in armor that easily weighed twice as much as me...and he carried himself like someone accustomed to being *obeyed*.

The honor guard immediately folded to one knee, thumping their chests. But it was the goblin I took my cues from—a fellow slave. He utterly prostrated himself, falling face-first to the packed dirt. So, I did the same. He might have pegged me for a stupid human, but I knew how to blend in when the situation called for it.

The captain of the honor guard, a pensive orc named Kof who'd lost an eye some years back, rose from his genuflection and addressed the head honcho. "I present Droko the Sage of the Two Swords Clan. Praise Ul-Rott."

I peeked up from the ground as this Ul-Rott character regarded the new shaman through narrowed eyes. "Formerly of the Two Swords Clan," said the chieftain. "Spoils of war. He belongs to us now. Woe to anyone who'd try to stake a claim on him."

"None would dare go back on a deal with Ul-Rott," Gargle immediately agreed–sickening toady.

Men in power tend to enjoy groveling…but the Red Hand chieftain already had the measure of Gargle. His gaze skimmed the guard and settled instead on Droko. He sized up the new shaman and gestured for him to come forward. "You're younger than I expected–though anyone seems like a stripling compared to Taruut. The most promising acolyte in generations–that's what everyone's saying about you. So, tell me, young shaman. What makes you so special?"

Most men I knew would not have hesitated to sing their own praises. But the new guy met the chieftain's gaze, held it for an uncomfortable moment, and after a long pause, said, "I suppose we'll find out."

Ul-Rott barked out a laugh. "Well said. A shaman wouldn't be a shaman if he made any promises he couldn't guarantee. What was your name, again?"

"Droko."

"Droko," the chieftain repeated.

"A common name in my clan. My...*former* clan."

Ul-Rott grunted. "Maybe we should call you Droko the Cautious. Regardless, your first order of business is to handle Taruut's burial rites. Old man could barely hold his own dick to piss. But he served this clan since my father was too small to lift a sword, and no effort will be spared."

"As you wish," Droko said stiffly. He was nowhere near as easy in his own skin as Taruut had been. Then again, Taruut's skin was saggy enough to accommodate a lot more ease.

The chieftain seemed eager to leave the arrangements in Droko's hands—I had the sense he'd much rather vanquish another clan than say a prayer. He turned on his heel to march off toward his sprawling lodge. Kof motioned for the rest of the honor guard to return to the caves. But even as they regained their feet, Ul-Rott turned back and said, "I expect you to have the shaman's crypt ready to receive Taruut in three days."

The one-eyed captain shifted. "No one knows where the tomb is," he murmured.

Ul-Rott narrowed his eyes. "What?"

Kof shrugged helplessly. "When Taruut died, he took that secret with him."

The chieftain made a negligent gesture encompassing the entire feather-bedecked enclave. "Why do we have a shaman if he can't make the ancestors speak? This is your problem, not mine. Find the crypt. Make it ready." He gave Droko a stern parting look. "And it had better be perfect."

5

DROKO

How the chieftain spoke to me—looked me right in the eye—and failed to see I was no shaman, I'll never know. Maybe claims of his cunning and prowess were exaggerated. Or maybe he'd seen through me already and was simply toying with me.

Or maybe he was a pragmatic orc who knew that appearances were all that mattered, and even a false shaman was better than no shaman at all.

Either way, this was my first test—the crypt must be ready in three days.

The crypt whose location was unknown.

My commander back home would tell me to be like the hunter stalking his prey. Watch and wait, and only strike when the time is right. But at the moment, I felt less like a hunter and more like a wounded buck leaving a blood trail in the undergrowth. One that was sure to be spotted.

There was nowhere to hide now. So I'd better start acting the hunter. "Ul-Rott the Spinecrusher has set us a task," I announced to the honor guards who'd accompanied me to the square. "We must waste no time in carrying out his orders."

The men shuffled awkwardly, and I recalled that they were unaccustomed to a shaman who could walk unassisted.

The captain, Kof, had placed himself at the top position, at my empty sword hand—my dominant hand. A true shaman would have no use for a sword. His honor guard would strike down any threat. As for me—I'd rather do the striking myself. The spot on either hip where my blades normally hung felt far too light, and the staff I carried would shatter if I ever used it against steel.

"Assign the marching order," I told him—but it was Gorgul, his lieutenant, who responded.

"Slaves bring up the rear," he said...and I was surprised to realize I also felt exposed without the goblin beside me. Even though Crespash had no claws or fangs, he'd gladly shove an attacker's eye in with the stump of his thumb, given half the chance.

Not that there was anything to fear inside the walls of this village...which was supposedly *my* village, now.

As we trooped back toward the shamanic cave, Crespash immediately broke rank and scampered up to grab my attention. "Has it not been a great while since you've eaten, oh Droko the Sage?" He jerked his head at the communal dining hall. It was laid out differently than the one I'd grown up with, but a mess hall is a mess hall. When I was still a child, I sat at my father's table. But I still recalled the pride I felt squatting among the men and slurping down my first bowl of gristly stew from the common pot.

Before I could reply, Gorgul answered Crespash with a whack to the thigh with the butt of his spear. Any lower and the goblin would have lost a kneecap. I wasn't the only one who'd need to play a role here. Goblins don't understand re-spect until it's beaten into them—and even then, they tend to forget. He'd become too familiar with me over the years. This was a good reminder of the order of things.

"The slave will prepare my food," I said, though Crespash was such a foul cook he'd probably manage to fumigate the caves by the time my dinner was done. "The human slave," I amended.

Kof, the one-eyed orc, said, "As the head of the honor guard, I am responsible for your life. That duty should fall to me." I leveled him a look, and he retracted the complaint. "As you wish."

A captain should not capitulate so quickly—even to his su-perior. There was something going on within the guard. Had Taruut known, or was it only obvious to a soldier like me?

"In the meantime," I said, "you will give the human proper clothing—and I will go and, er...prepare to locate the tomb."

I could hardly get back to my new private chambers—and away from the guardsmen—soon enough. I squatted gingerly, rubbing my aching head, while Crespash flung himself down in the old shaman's sedan chair. "Well," he said sarcastically, "that was quite the convincing lie. No one would ever question you were a shaman."

"What would you have me tell them?"

"Any mumbo jumbo would do. No doubt a real shaman would find the crypt by working his magic. Though, I con-fess, I'm not exactly clear on how he'd go about the task. Consult the stars? Pray to the ancestors? Sacrifice a chicken?"

"How would I know?" I grumbled. "Our shaman would never speak to anyone but his acolytes, let alone do any rit-uals where the rest of us could watch."

"Then definitely see about that chicken."

"Would you stop thinking about food for once and do something useful? If they find me out, you're as good as dead yourself."

"Calm down, Droko the Sage. If your supposed mentor was secretive, it stands to reason that you'd be just as opaque. So stay in your chambers performing your 'rituals' while I go figure out where this crypt might be."

The suggestion sounded suspiciously helpful. But goblins love nothing better than skulking through winding cave passages in the dark—especially if they could find an escape route that let out somewhere beyond the village walls. "If you think I'm stupid enough to just allow you to—"

"What's the alternative, hm? Going to the chieftain three days from now and telling him you haven't even found the crypt, let alone made it ready? Look, Third Son, I'll make you a deal. If I find a way out of this place, then obviously, I'm taking it. But if I find the crypt first, I'll tell you where it is. One good 'prophecy' should set you up for a long time to come."

Only a fool would trust a goblin's promise. Though what other choice did I have?

I said, "If anyone asks what you're doing, be vague. Just say you're on a mission from the shaman."

"Why would anyone ask?" He flashed a gummy grin. "They won't even know I was there."

Once he did find that crypt, then what? If only I could glean some clue among the old shaman's belongings—anything to make it seem like I knew what I was doing. I took stock of the chamber. Shelves crowded the room, stuffed full of crystals, strange stones, and bundles of various herbs. Not a single scroll. I picked up a clump of greenery and gave it a sniff. My eyes watered. I had no idea what it was. In fact, the same could be said for everything else. Object after object, I turned things over, racking my brain for some notion of the purpose these things might serve.

I recognized nothing.

I'd worked my way around to a huge collection of stoppered vials. None of them were labeled. I sniffed one, then another. From what I could tell, the tinctures smelled mostly of the alcohol used to distill them. I was just about to admit to myself that I couldn't name a single thing in that room... when I unstoppered a bottle and finally recognized the scent of pepper.

And then the curtain rustled in my doorway, and a human face poked through the gap. "Dinner's served."

The scent had come from the food—not the tincture. I stoppered the vial and motioned him in.

The guards had dressed the human male in a simple linen outfit, the sort that a young recruit, too small for armor, would be given his first night at the longhouse. Though the human was an adult, it was far too big. He held a platter of steaming goat, surrounded by roasted tubers and studded with peppercorns. The platter itself was plain, but the meal looked fit for a chieftain's table. "You prepared this with your own hands?" I demanded.

"Why is that so hard to believe?" A smile tugged at the corner of the human's mouth. "I'm told my hands are very talented, indeed."

He spoke like Crespash. Not with a toothless goblin lisp, obviously—but in a maddening, indirect tone hinting that something crucial was being left unsaid. It was not the orc way.

Then again, he was clearly not an orc. My gaze landed on the delicate hollow at the base of his smooth, pale throat. I lingered there for a moment, then forced myself to look away, swallowing hard.

I shoved some twigs and bundles aside to clear room on a table. "Put it down."

Archie walked around the table so I was at his back—as if the soft white throat wasn't vulnerable enough—then placed the tray down with a slight wiggle in his rump. Over his shoulder, he tossed the words, "Anything else I can do for you?"

"Eat."

He turned and glanced pointedly at my crotch before meeting my eyes. "Pardon me?"

The caves were full of herbs and potions. *Poisonous* herbs and potions. And the sharp smell of pepper could mask any of them. "You heard me. Eat."

But if my command surprised the human, he didn't show it.

He smiled, a secret light in his eyes. He took up a tuber and brought it to his lips, then tenderly bit off a piece like he was eating from my hand. His gaze flicked up to meet mine as he chewed it with his blunt human teeth. I felt the heat of that look throughout my entire body.

His lips shone with grease. I couldn't tear my eyes away.

"Delicious," he murmured.

The sound of orcish voices carried from elsewhere in the caves, reminding me that any sense of us being alone together was nothing but an illusion. I grabbed my eating knife from my belt, speared a few morsels from various parts of the plate, then aimed the tip at that tender hollow in the human's throat. "Eat," I repeated.

With an easy shrug, he took a bit of goat between his fingers, slipped the meat from the knife, and ate it...all the while staring me unflinchingly in the eye. "Anything else you'd like me to do?" he asked lightly as his gaze fell to my lips. "Perhaps I should breathe your air."

Something inside me shivered and I choked down a fierce knot of need. "Drink," I growled as I poured a cup from an earthenware jug, then placed it into his hand. The human accepted the cup and tilted it back, savoring every last drop with a contented sigh.

I couldn't stop myself from admiring the way his throat moved as he swallowed, how his eyes had suddenly mellowed with pleasure, and that faint, knowing smile when he caught me staring.

It was too much. This human unsettled me like no one ever had. His attitude, his scent, the uncanny sense that he knew what I was thinking—it was almost as if I was bewitched.

"That's all," I said, as firmly as I could manage, my voice brittle with tension. "Now, leave me."

Archie paused, treating me to one more lingering look before he finally obeyed.

Alone, I stood in the emptiness of the cluttered room. My breath came in shallow gasps, as though I'd just scaled a precarious bluff in search of stormsilver. But the precipice I now found myself upon was twice as steep...and far more dangerous.

6

ARCHIE

I got a real kick out of riling up the new shaman. And why not? He was unexpectedly young and strong and...dare I say it? Even handsome. In his own way. For an orc.

I supposed I wouldn't have thought so, back in Wildwood. But the majority of the faces I saw nowadays were green.

Maybe the color was starting to grow on me.

Or maybe it was the hint of decency I sensed beneath his brusque exterior when he had me unchained. Probably just wishful thinking on my part...but at the very least, I suspected there was tolerance.

Couldn't say the same for Gargle.

I've never understood why some bullies feel the need to pick on the underdogs. There's a saying in Wildwood: it's like squashing bugs in a basket. You'd think a big, strong orc wouldn't get off on poking and prodding an unarmed slave. But cruelty is its own reward, and Gargle was especially fond of rewarding himself. I'd have to be sure to keep out of his way.

Unfortunately, the only part of the caves I'd memorized

yet were the passages surrounding Taruut's chambers. The old man couldn't walk—and for the majority of my convalescence, neither could I. Caves are nothing like buildings, with square walls and level floors and everything the size you'd expect. Caves were built by nature, not people. Broad tunnels squeezed down to nothing. They twisted and turned and looped back on themselves. They might lead to a delightfully hot, if somewhat stinky, bath. Or they might end in a sharp drop into the earth too deep for the lantern beam to reach.

Still, hoping to keep out of the honor guards' way, I made sure my lantern was shuttered. Only the thinnest shaft of light peeked through to ensure I didn't tumble down a bottomless pit. I was putting some distance between the guards and me when I came upon a passageway I'd never taken before, and the moment I came to the far end, I knew I was somewhere *different*. My skin prickled and the small hairs at the back of my neck stood on end. I'd never put much stock in so-called magic...but the chamber at the end of the passage definitely felt like a place of power. A slick-looking golden sheen coated the walls. It shimmered like honey in the faint glow of the lantern. Preserved things were pressed into its surface—leaves, roots, animal bones—all frozen in time.

"It's amber," said a lisping voice, and I whirled around, the single light beam dancing wildly. Crespash stood in the tunnel, blocking my way out. And while he might've looked slight and scrawny compared to the huge, bulky orcs, now that the two of us were alone, he was clearly more than a match for me.

I suspected my normal weapon—flirtation—wouldn't

do me much good against the goblin. I did my best to look wide-eyed and innocent, though I wasn't sure if that would impress a creature with eyes that took up half his head.

The goblin slunk into the chamber, feet utterly soundless on the crumbly stone floor as he dragged a stumpy finger along the chamber wall. "Tunneling through rock, you'll find pockets like this on occasion. Rooms hollowed out by long-ago trees…trees as big as a whole village, with roots wider than a road. You'd think a goblin tunneler would be pleased to come across such a find. After all, that's fewer tons of rock they'll need to move."

He'd eased up beside me—and obviously, I'd seen him coming—but I hadn't accounted for the absurd reach of his lanky arms. A cloudy membrane flicked over his bulbous eyes just as he snatched the lantern from me and threw the shutter wide. I held up a hand, squinting through my fingers, as the whole chamber blazed with reflected orange light.

"Amber might be prized by the jewelsmiths," Crespash said, "but if all the creatures stuck here aren't an ill omen…I don't know what is."

He gestured with the lantern, and my gaze fell on a figure stuck in the resin. I'd seen gems with small insects fixed inside—an ant, even a spider—but nothing like this. Within the glistening wall, right beside my head, a frog was trapped in time. It was a huge specimen nearly as long as my forearm, frozen mid-leap. As if maybe was trying to escape. If only he'd been quick enough.

The goblin tossed the lantern back at me, and I scrambled to catch it as it guttered wildly. *He doesn't care if it goes out*, I realized. He could see in the dark.

"You know a lot about caves," I said, hoping flattery might

work where flirtation was clearly unwelcome.

He spat a hiss of a laugh. "I'm a goblin. That's like saying rocks are hard. Even my simplest cousins can tell shale from slate. But I'm far from simple...."

The membrane peeled back from his eye, revealing a glistening gray orb of an iris with a black slit pupil in the center.

"...and I see how you're trying to get under Droko's skin."

"I have no idea what you mean."

"Deny it all you want, but I know a troublemaker when I see one. Orcs are predictable creatures. Born and bred to follow the rules. Not goblins. We're well aware the only way to get ahead is to double-cross your enemies before they do the same to you."

Despite the warmth of the caves—and a burn I'd just acquired catching the damn lantern—I shivered.

"Let me tell you something, little human." The goblin stepped forward, and I took a matching step back, well aware now of his longer reach. A hand shot out and I bent backward to avoid getting smacked, but he was only fanning his finger-stumps in front of my eyes for emphasis. "The only thing standing between me and a gaggle of bloodthirsty orcs is Droko. Without him, I'm screwed. If they take it in their minds that I need discipline, there's nothing left for them to cut off but my dick...or my head. And I'm not willing to lose either one. Understand?"

I swallowed hard. "I'm a slave, same as you. We'd be better off working together."

"If you think I'm gullible enough to call you my ally just because you're not an orc, think again."

Before I could protest, he fit himself into a crack in the wall I hadn't even seen. He gave off a grunt of effort, contorting as his joints popped. And then he was gone, and the chamber of amber was quiet, save for the hiss of my lantern, and the beating of my own heart.

The goblin wouldn't help me? Fine. I didn't trust goblins anyway—and I've always found that the only one I could depend on was myself. So, where did that leave me?

Escape was out of the question—if the orcs didn't hunt me down in the woods beyond the gates, wild animals certainly would. And if Bess was to be believed, the handsome young shaman might be inclined to extend his protection to me...if I served him well. It wasn't enough to kneel at his feet, either.

Anyone can suck cock.

I would need to make myself *indispensable*. Not just making Droko's meals and tasting his food, but being the extra hand he never knew he needed.

Not only was the fresh, young acolyte new, but he came from another clan entirely—whereas I had spent a lot of time with Taruut, just him and me, with no guards in sight. I'm a quick learner. I'd watched him sort through his ingredients, navigating by touch. And I'd witnessed his healing rituals first-hand.

I was the perfect guy to show Droko the ropes.

But then there was Gargle. From the moment I'd opened my eyes in the steam room, I could tell he had it in for me. And if Droko began taking advice from him, I would be the one who was screwed.

I'd just need to keep Droko's attention focused where it belonged—on me.

7

DROKO

How could a room so full of things be so utterly useless?

I sifted through the chaos of Taruut's collection, desperate for anything I could use to prop up the falsehood I had to perpetuate. Every object I touched mocked my ignorance. Somewhere in this clutter lay the proof of what a true shaman should know—and with every passing moment, my inability to recognize it brought me closer to exposure. Each meaningless relic only hammered home the truth—I was an imposter surrounded by evidence of my own deception. And soon, I would be found out.

In my father's house, when the shaman of the Two Swords clan refused the chieftain's invitation to join us at the dinner table, his messenger often claimed he was deep in meditation. My father scoffed at such things, of course. Never in front of a member of the shaman's household...but he clearly put no stock in the shaman's ways.

I can think of no worse punishment for an orc than doing nothing. If I were forced to sit there like a lump waiting for 'wisdom' to rain down on me, I'd go mad.

I had presumed that claim was an exaggeration.

Now, though, pawing uselessly through all the tinctures and unguents, bones and branches, I realized exactly how much I dreaded the thought of sitting here idly in hopes of finding that burial chamber. Idleness is simply not the orcish way.

And yet, this "meditation" was likely the only shamanic practice I'd be able to mimic with any chance of success.

I squatted with my back to the wall and tried to meditate. It was useless. My thoughts kept straying to Archie and his inviting throat, his lips slick with grease, his eyes full of secrets and unspoken promises as he watched me watch him eat....

Back at my home clan, from my bunk in the longhouse, I would often hear other soldiers trading stories in the dark. They'd go on about which of the village girls would have the tightest cunt. Or brag about having their dick sucked by one of the kitchen slaves. Or wager whether the mongrel washerwoman inherited her twat from her ogre or human side.

I never joined in the banter. I was betrothed to Farya, the daughter of a chieftain, and that was all that mattered to me. I'd always thought others were fools for their obsession with rutting.

Until now.

Footfalls sounded in the hall. I sniffed the air, scenting a male orc a moment before the footsteps went still, just outside my door. "What is it?" I demanded.

The captain of my honor guard—the one-eyed orc named Kof—pushed the curtain of dangling bones aside and entered, kneeling before me. "Droko the Sage, my spear is yours. I've come to see if the room is to your liking. Taruut collected many things over the years. I thought you might need help with—"

"Tell me something," I cut in.

Kof dipped his head. "I live to serve."

"Taruut had plenty of guards, but no acolytes. Why? Was he expecting to be attacked in his own home?"

"Taruut must have had his reasons," the captain said vaguely. "But he didn't share them with me." He went quiet, then, gazing at the shamanic oddments cluttering the room with an unreadable expression in his single eye.

Kof was perhaps a dozen years older than me, with proud tusks, broad shoulders, a deep voice, and a scar from his browbone to his jaw with a divot where the missing eye used to be. He was dressed as all the rest of the honor guard, in light armor trimmed with sacred green feathers. But unlike the men under his command, he had a pensive way about him, a tendency to hesitate before he spoke.

His silence unsettled me. It wasn't the watchful quiet of a guard, but something deeper, more considering. He studied each of Taruut's things as if reading a story written in dust. Most orcs would have filled such silence with attempts to prove their worth to a new commander. Kof did not.

I'd been hoping for more information, but I couldn't press him to speak without risking exposure of my own ignorance.

Kof seemed more interested in the trinkets surrounding me than in my shamanic abilities—or lack thereof. But judging by the wear on his spear handle, he'd served Taruut quite a while. That made it all the more likely he would eventually notice I didn't have a clue what being a shaman entailed—even if he were to claim Taruut didn't confide in him...and he only observed the old shaman with one eye.

"There's...so much here." Kof's fingers traced the worn

leather of Taruut's sedan chair, his voice rough. "I could help clear some of it away. Make space for your things."

"Taruut's belongings stay," I said firmly, hoping to rid myself of the captain as soon as possible. Kof didn't challenge me—he wouldn't dare. But he did seem baffled by the statement. I added, "The dead are less likely to anger if we leave their possessions be until they're laid to rest."

Instead of backing away at the mention of spirits, Kof drew closer. His hand lingered on the chair, fingers brushing the wooden arm—worn smooth by years of the shaman's touch. Stroking it, he said, "I think Taruut knew the crypt wouldn't be found in his lifetime. He once told me, *The path lies unread until seen with knowing eyes.*"

"And what's that supposed to mean?"

"As far as I can tell—"

Kof's words died as heavy footsteps sounded in the hall, and Gorgul's shadow fell across the threshold.

"Droko the Sage," he barked out, genuflecting forcefully as his captain turned and strode from the chamber. Damn it. I'd need to be cautious around this one, too. "Your journey has been long, and yet your slave is nowhere to be found. Your waterskin is empty and your boots are caked with dust."

A situation the shaman of Two Swords would never have put up with. "I do not trouble myself with such insignificant worldly matters," I said quickly.

"Of course not. That's what those who serve you are for." It sounded like he'd bought my excuse. That was a relief. "Slaves require a firm hand," he went on. "I would be honored to oversee them so you don't need to."

Would my clan's shaman have delegated the task? Most likely. But Crespash could hardly scout for me with the guardsman breathing down his neck. "You don't get the measure of a man unless his scent is on your tongue. I will deal with my own slaves."

"As you wish." I suspected Gorgul was disappointed he couldn't curry favor with me, though like any good soldier, he didn't show it.

I motioned for him to go, and as he did, the bone curtain in the doorway rattled. "And the lack of privacy here isn't helping my concentration," I called after him. "Tell the other guards I'm not to be disturbed."

Maybe he'd manage to do that—and maybe not. A shift of power always left underlings jockeying for position. So I wasn't exactly surprised when moments later, yet another man dared approach…though the scent of him was definitely not orcish.

"Droko the Sage." Archie paused in the doorway and performed the necessary obeisance, tapping the floor with one knee. No doubt he was usually graceful, but the bundle he carried made the move awkward.

"Did Gorgul send you?"

"Not at all." He bustled his way in. "I just thought you might have need of a few things."

All of the tables and shelves were full of shamanic nonsense, so he placed his bundle on the empty sedan chair instead. He opened the sackcloth to reveal several white tallow candles, a heavy tinderbox, and a jug of wine.

"I didn't ask for this."

"Maybe not." Archie hoisted the jug, eyes sparkling. "But I've been looking forward to my tasting duties."

If the human thought to lower my inhibitions with something as weak as wine, he'd be disappointed. I grabbed the extra candles to stow them near the sconces, only to find their supply nearly gone, and the spot where they'd normally be kept held only a single, brittle candle stump and a few hunks of wax.

"As you see," Archie purred. "I can be very...useful."

Obviously, he was hinting at the sorts of things my bunkmates bragged about in the dark—a notion from which I forcefully steered my thoughts away. But perhaps he truly could be useful to me...just not quite in the way he expected.

"Tell me," I commanded. "How often did the shaman Taruut meditate?"

The question surprised him. "Hard to say."

"So much for your usefulness. I doubt you were anywhere near as close to the old shaman as you want me to believe."

"Hold on, now. Maybe I am the new kid in town, and maybe I was pretty busy coughing up my own lungs—but Taruut and I did spend quite a bit of time together. Who else would've mopped my brow or spooned broth down my throat? Certainly not Gar—er, Gorgul."

"You mean to tell me that the most venerable shaman this clan has ever known lavished all his personal attention on you? To what purpose?"

Archie shrugged helplessly. "Taruut never explained to me—or to anyone else—why he was so determined to keep me alive. *It was foretold.* That's all he would say."

If this slave was so important to the old shaman, perhaps he could be of use to me as well. "Kof shared another of Taruut's riddles with me: *The path lies unread until seen with knowing eyes.*"

"How delightfully cryptic." Archie's lips curved into a smile at his own wordplay. "Speaking of knowing eyes...." His insolent gaze locked with mine.

"In the Two Swords clan, an orc would never tolerate such games from a slave."

Archie wasn't cowed in the least. In fact, he only eased closer, voice dropping to a sultry whisper. "And yet...here you are, playing right along."

The human smelled nothing whatsoever like an orc. I backed away to quell the temptation to sniff him. "Find out what that prophecy means. Watch Kof, listen to the guards, do whatever you need to do—but don't get caught. Or you may find yourself serving a much harsher master."

Archie set off, finally, to do my bidding, though his human scent lingered long after he was gone. Maybe I was foolish to think a human slave to be of any help. Humans don't understand their place in the world. I'd be better off enlisting the help of Gorgul—at least he seemed eager to impress me. But before I could call him back, I was interrupted yet again as Crespash returned.

"I passed the human in the hall," he said without preamble, "though, of course, he didn't see me. What was he doing here again?"

"Bringing me that wine you've had your eye on. What difference is it to you?"

Crespash unstoppered the flagon, gave the wine a sniff, then shrugged and dumped it down his gullet. Smacking his lips, he said, "No doubt the boy's flattery is like honey to your ears, and his sky-colored eyes are full of promise. And who could blame you for needing some release after you were deprived of the wedding night you'd been anticipating since you were old enough to sprout hair on your balls? But you'll hardly have time to savor his sweet little pink cock if your head's on a stake."

8

ARCHIE

I'd been hoping to seduce Droko, not make myself his lackey. But if I could find a good vantage point to spy on the honor guard, I might learn something useful about that prophecy, though why Droko thought a common bedboy could succeed where a mystical orcish shaman couldn't was beyond me. Still, he'd asked, and I wasn't about to disappoint my best chance at surviving with my head intact.

The trick would be figuring out somewhere I could watch the guards without being spotted myself.

I searched through the caves, looking for hidden passages or secret overlooks. The caves were treacherous—a place of secrets, dank and dark and filled with potential hazards. Most of the passageways reeked of sulfur, though that was probably for the best. It meant the honor guard wouldn't be able to *smell* me while I watched them.

I shuddered.

I'd have to be careful around the honor guard. If Gargle had his way, I'd be done for. He'd been eager to be rid of me once Taruut died and the old man's protection with him—and he'd be twice as eager to see me gone if I landed myself in Droko's good graces. Finding a safe place to observe them without being seen was crucial.

I might not know much about orcs, but I was no stranger to a ruthless rivalry. On a slow night at the brothel, ten boys would all vie for the attention of the same paying man... and only the most cutthroat among us would wind up with enough coin for a meal and a bed.

Gargle wasn't the only one who had it in for me, either. That creepy goblin wouldn't shed any tears for me if I wound up on the wrong end of a spear.

But the memory of him cramming his body through impossibly small cracks *had* got me to thinking...maybe I hadn't been searching these passages nearly as well as I'd thought.

I searched. But now I examined the cave walls more carefully, and eventually I spotted a crescent-shaped gap I'd initially taken for a shadow. It was barely as wide as my hips turned sideways. I contorted myself and pushed my way through, gritting my teeth as the rough edges scraped against me.

Greedy rock clawed at my clothes and hair. I exhaled hard, taking only shallow sips of breath in hopes of making myself smaller, but it was no use. The walls felt as if they were closing all around me—like I'd wedged myself into the maw of the cliffside and would soon be swallowed whole. Even worse, as I dithered about turning back, I started to second-guess which direction I'd even come from.

If I meet my maker, I thought, at least I'll die standing. I was crammed in so tight, there'd be nowhere for me to fall. Not exactly how I'd planned to die...but I supposed it was better than starving to death once I was too old for the flesh trade.

I was running through all the worse ways I could have perished—the dick pox, for instance—when I realized I felt the air stirring at my right hand. If it wasn't just my fading mind playing tricks on me, maybe I wasn't so turned around after all. I drew a steadying breath, then exhaled solidly and crammed myself toward the breeze.

It took a few tries, but eventually, I staggered out of the rock crevice and into a man-made chamber, with straight walls, a level floor, and a cavernous ceiling. A shaft of dim light shone down through a narrow gap high overhead, where a full moon rode the night sky.

I hadn't expected to choke up from the sight of the sky. It stirred up dangerous hopes I couldn't afford.

I shut them down. Wanting what you can't have never ends well.

I tore my gaze from the hole in the ceiling and scanned the chamber. There'd been a doorway, once, cut into the wall across from me, but the passage was now caved in. And a half dozen still figures lay upon low stone biers in two neat rows of three, flat on their backs with their hands folded on their chests.

I sucked in a breath. Maybe I'd turned out to be pretty useless as a spy...but wouldn't Droko be thrilled when I told him I'd found the crypt of the shamans? Or, at any rate, as thrilled as orcs allowed themselves to get.

I set down my lantern and crept cautiously forward. But even before I reached the bodies, I could tell that they were too small to be orcs—orcs of the fully grown variety, anyhow. As I rounded the figures, I saw that they hadn't simply seemed short because I'd been looking at them from an odd angle. They truly were short. Even shorter than me—but easily three or four times as wide.

Whatever they were...talk about *girth*. But they weren't orcs. Not at all.

My shoulders slumped. Just how many crypts were hidden in these endless caves? And what kind of creatures were these, anyhow? I'd thought I'd had the "eyes to see" something to help Droko, but no. I was just a useless bedboy nobody here even wanted.

Why should I care about failing an orc—one who, despite all my best flirting, still saw me as nothing more than a slave?

The sensible thing would be to do as I'd been told and eavesdrop on the honor guard. But I'd never been very sensible, and my curiosity was already getting the better of me. After all, how often did you stumble across...whatever these things were?

I paused, weighing my options. Returning to my spy duties might please Droko, potentially securing me a safer position. But this crypt...it wasn't the one we needed, true, but it might prove to be *something*. Something hidden, something valuable. The shaft in the ceiling taunted me with a glimpse of freedom, even if it was out of reach. And this place could be my secret refuge if things went south.

Cautiously, I approached the closest bier. I would have expected the corpses to be rotten, but they were incredibly well-preserved. Maybe even petrified, as if the atmosphere of the caves had conspired to protect them from the elements, although that protection would no longer be appreciated.

Even in the meager light, I could tell these dead guys weren't orcs or goblins—and they definitely weren't humans. They had eyes, nose, and mouth (presumably, under their big, flowing beards) but aside from that, their faces looked like no men I'd ever seen. The noses were broad, the brows heavy, and the eyes set wide in the skull. I'm not sure what color they used to be, back when they were up walking around. Now, their flesh looked stony, almost like sculpture, and their garments were covered in a fine sifting of limestone dust. I could have taken them for skillfully made statues, if not for the dusty topknots and beards that were clearly made of hair. Whatever they were, they'd been here for ages, completely undisturbed.

Which meant whatever they were buried with was fair game.

Some people think it's bad luck to steal from a corpse—and those people have never had to sell their bodies for a crust of stale bread. The way I see it, the dead have no use for their jewelry and baubles, and someone's eventually bound to come along and plunder those treasures. That someone might as well be me.

I took up my lantern and gave the dead guys a more thorough assessment. Five of them were buried in plain, serviceable clothing. Mostly light leather armor, cracked with age. Well-made, but without any tooling or ornamentation. But the sixth dead guy must've been their leader. His boots were fancier. The buckles on his chest piece were etched with geometric designs. And the dusty ring on his forefinger would bring in some good coin, even if the gemstone in the setting turned out to be common.

I'd been telling myself there was no point dreaming of escape—the Wastelands would kill me as surely as the orcs would. But that ring...that ring could change everything. Such a fine piece of jewelry could buy more than just a meal or a bed for the night. It could buy a whole new life, far from stinky caves and nasty honor guards. *Far from Droko*, a voice whispered in my head, but I pushed that thought aside.

Unfortunately, that ring wasn't merely stuck tight...it was bonded with his finger. Not only did the bodies look like statues, they felt hard as granite. I'd been expecting some resistance, sure. But no matter how I tugged and twisted, that finger didn't budge.

I cast around for something to help me pry up the finger, and my gaze fell on the dead guy's scabbard. No idea what it says about me that I only had eyes for a jewel when a weapon was right in front of me. A heavy ring might buy my passage on a caravan—but I could hardly expect a caravan to troop through the orcish caves just in case a slave was hoping for a ride. Before I could spend any ill-gotten gains, I'd need a way out.

And that meant I'd also need to fight.

Not that I stood any chance of landing a blow on one of those spear-toting bullies, mind you. But cutting someone's throat while they slept....

I'd never killed a man. But to keep myself out of the slave pit...maybe I could.

I pushed away the thought as I reached for the scabbard. I'd expected the sword to be cemented in place like the ring, but with a determined wiggle, it came free. Unfortunately, it was too big to fit in my belt and far too heavy for me to wield one-handed. Heck, it was hard to lift the thing even with both. Even if the guards miraculously ignored the fact that I was dragging a massive sword along behind me, I doubted I would get in more than a single swing before one of them put a spear through my belly.

Moonlight shifted and I glanced up at the hole in the high

ceiling. Maybe I could fit through that shaft—if I somehow sprouted wings. So close, yet so far. Still, it did give me hope that maybe there was another way out of these caves after all—one that the orcs didn't know about because they couldn't navigate the tight passages. If I did find an exit, I'd prefer to have something other than my bedroom skills to trade.

Maybe I could still salvage the ring.

Anyone with a lick of sense wouldn't dream of using a fine blade to hack at a petrified corpse, but if that was the only use I had for the sword, so be it.

I managed to raise the sword. It was a lot heavier than I'd thought. I didn't swing at the stony finger, so much as simply allow the ponderous blade to fall. I'd expected a loud clang. The chipping of metal. Maybe even sparks. What I didn't anticipate was the sword falling straight through, as if the stony man was made of fresh meringue.

A huge hunk sheared off and crumbled to the floor. I hadn't just severed the petrified finger—I'd shattered the ring, and taken off part of the bier while I was at it. Never in my life had I seen a blade so sharp—and when I inspected it to see how much damage I'd foolishly done to the edge, there wasn't a nick to be seen.

Screw the ring. This sword was my ticket out of here—not to fight my way out, but to sell it once I snuck off into the night.

While the sword was easily the most valuable thing I'd ever encountered, I wasn't about to leave the ring behind. Even in pieces—and even if it was silver, not gold—I could trade it for something. And it would be a heck of a lot easier to hide.

Going by touch, I sifted through the grit and rubble, doing my best not to imagine the stone I'd just fondled was actually a finger. I was about to cut my losses when I glanced up at the stone corpse and saw the gleam of metal where his hand (and a hunk of the bier) had been cut away.

The dead guy's hand had been covering a *knife*. The big ol' sword had nicked the pommel, but the rest of it might be intact. There was a sheath, meticulously hand-sewn from black leather and edged with lengths of rawhide stitches, built into the guy's vest. It was just large enough to carry a bone-handled knife and nothing else.

I worked the blade free. It was long as my hand, and curved like a fang, with a satin edge that seemed to call for blood. I had no idea if it was made for battle or for cleaning the dirt from under its owner's fingernails, but I knew one thing: between the sword and the knife, I had something far more valuable than some old ring.

I had a chance.

My loose linen pants could easily hide the dagger. I cut a strip of cloth from the hem to strap the blade to my thigh, then resumed my search for whatever was left of the ring. I was scanning the rubble with my lantern opened wider when my fingers closed on something small and hard. I brought it closer to the light, my breath catching as I saw a deep blue gemstone, about the size of my thumbnail. I'm no jeweler, so I couldn't tell what I was looking at—but I knew for sure it was one big stone. I quickly pocketed my ticket to a whole new life. Assuming I could get out of this cave alive, of course.

As I straightened up, ready to make my exit, I noticed a discolored bit of parchment sticking out from beneath the bier.

A scroll.

The path lies unread until seen with knowing eyes.

Well, damn. I'd been looking for a literal path. But obviously, I should've had my eyes peeled for a map!

With bated breath, I teased it out from under the bier. It had been there for some time. The edges were frayed and stained with mildew, and simply looking at it made me dizzy with anticipation. Droko would be so thrilled when he saw it.

Not that I *cared*, of course, since I wouldn't be sticking around. I had a solid plan. The gemstone would be enough to grab a ride on the next caravan I came across, the dagger would protect me, and the sword could set me up for life in one of the border settlements...maybe even in The Fortifications themselves.

Still, I couldn't help but be curious.

I brought the scroll over to the lantern and carefully unfurled the parchment.

It was no map. Just a bunch of weird markings.

So much for my "knowing" eyes.

I pondered the marks, feeling stupid. I'm not as good with letters as I am with figures, so I wasn't even sure whether I was looking at words or some kind of random tally. If it was writing, it hadn't been done in any script I knew. Maybe this was how orcs wrote things down—different from the common letters I'd learned in the pleasure houses. Either way, it wouldn't help me impress Droko. Just another dead end.

No matter. I wasn't planning to stay long enough to bask in the strapping young shaman's appreciation, anyway. Maybe I couldn't reach the air shaft. But now that I knew I could shove myself through tiny gaps like a goblin, no doubt I'd soon find another. One I could actually get to.

The narrow passage back didn't seem quite so daunting on my return trip, even dragging the heavy sword in one hand and hefting the lantern in the other. The comfort was in knowing that the tight squeeze didn't go on forever. Before the crack opened out into a broader tunnel, I used the precious sword to carve a ledge into the living rock of the cave. The niche was both well away from prying eyes and easy to grab, in a gap that I could get to without skinning myself alive, but where a burly orc could never hope to follow.

I was shocked when even without the momentum of a clumsy swing, the sword pushed through the rock like the cave walls were made of stale bread.

Maybe the sword could be good for more than just barter.

The shaft overhead in the burial chamber had seemed impossibly out of reach earlier. But now, with this incredible sword in hand, I saw a new possibility. I didn't need a pair of wings or another exit. I could cut stairs into the wall and *carve* my way out of this place for good. I simply needed to gather a few supplies, first.

Oh, who was I kidding? I couldn't leave without seeing the look on Droko's face when I showed him that scroll.

9

DROKO

I should have been worn out from my long trek to the Red Hand village and my even longer day pretending to be something I was not...but still, I slept fitfully in the strange, hot chamber. It was too quiet without the snores and snuffles of my fellow soldiers, and the air reeked of sulfur. I had dreams that I was stuck in a dark stone room, the walls smooth and vertical. I scrabbled at them to try and find a way out, but they were polished to a sheen like glass, and my nails made an eerie skritching noise against them....

Which, I realized as I opened my eyes, was just the sound of Crespash vigorously scratching his balls with a dry twig. "Is that from my sacred staff?" I asked.

"Don't blame me." He tossed the twig into the brazier. "Take a man's claws...he's forced to make do."

I sat up and shook my waterskin—empty—then glanced at my mud-caked boots. Gorgul was right about my slave's lack of attention. Hopefully that meant the goblin had fared better with the task I'd actually charged him to do. "Did you find the shaman's crypt?"

"Obviously not, otherwise I wouldn't be sitting here watching you mumble to yourself in your sleep. Did your bunkmates back at the longhouse put up with that?"

"Keep your voice down." I scented the air to be sure we were alone. The goblin was too blase about me being a soldier. "There's no privacy here, and the tunnels make the sound carry."

I stood and crossed the room to check my "staff," the tree branch we'd hastily decorated on our trek to the Red Hand Clan. Staves are normally made by carefully selecting the proper wood, of a grain that is neither too tight nor too loose, honing it down, then curing and hardening the final product. Once hardened, the wood would be exactingly sanded and oiled, and with enough use, it would eventually fit itself to the shape of the holder's grasp.

This thing we'd created was hardly stronger than the smoldering twig. In the forest, it had seemed passable. But if anyone took a better look at it, we'd be in real trouble.

"This whole ruse is a single false move away from falling apart," I told Crespash, "And you're in as much hot water as me. If you don't find that crypt, this clan will stake your head right beside mine."

"And that's if they even give me a stake of my very own. Most likely they'll just stack us together like a shish kebab."

"This is no joke."

"Indeed, it's not. I covered at least ten miles of passages last night, and there was nary a crypt to be seen. Though I did find your little human sniffing around—"

"He was following my orders."

"Oh? How can you be so sure? You weren't there, after all...."

He trailed off at the sound of approaching footsteps.

Crespash might love a good argument, but his instinct for survival is well-honed. Gorgul presented himself in my doorway with all the proper greetings, then announced, "My men and I have been searching all night for the crypt, Droko the Sage—"

Crespash muttered in my ear, "Loudly enough to wake every last dead shaman."

"—and we haven't found it yet. But—" the guard hastened to add, "I did discover something you will find very useful. Follow me, and I'll show you."

I waved him back into the hall. "I will join you in a moment."

He retreated as I ordered, though not very far. I felt Crespash's slobber against my neck as he leaned in to whisper, "He's leading you off to the headsman already?"

"Doubtful. If the chieftain gave the order, Gorgul would carry it out himself, here, on the spot."

The goblin scoffed. "What are you saying—you actually trust this brute?"

"We are orcs, not goblins. We know our place in the world. Gorgul has nothing to gain by seeing me fail. If anything, he'd want to prove his worth to keep his position secure." I slipped on the ridiculous shamanic raiments we'd crafted on our way there. The leaves on the neckpiece were already crumbling. Leaving Crespash behind, I rejoined the lieutenant of my honor guard in the hall.

Gorgul led me deeper into the caves with a purposeful stride, and before long, a slither of unease crept up my spine. I'd been trained in the forest. I wasn't used to being underground. And the farther we went, the more I wondered if maybe Crespash had sensed something about the guard's motivations I'd been unwilling to see.

The passageway turned...then dead-ended. The perfect spot to trap me in an ambush. I tightened my grip on my makeshift staff. It creaked, and bits of bark sloughed off, scattering to the ground. Gorgul turned and smiled with great satisfaction.

I planted my feet, readying myself to dodge a spear, and flinched as he lunged....

Only to realize he'd folded humbly to one knee. He bowed his head and said, "I hope this tool will serve you well, Droko the Sage. It was Taruut's private meditation chamber. It hasn't seen use in decades—longer than any of the honor guard have served—because his sedan chair didn't fit through the passage. But a pair of my best men have spent the night readying it for your use."

Gorgul stood and shoved against the dead end, revealing that the wall was a stone that could be rolled aside. As he did, I let out a breath I'd been holding. Crespash might know caves...but he didn't know orcs. Not like I did. Gorgul could be trusted to serve the shaman. It was just a matter of making sure he thought that shaman was me.

I nodded my approval to Gorgul and stepped into the chamber he'd revealed. The lieutenant stood right outside the door, erect and proud, spear drawn and ready to impale any who tried to gain access without my permission.

The chamber was simple and utterly private. It was carved out of the rock walls with only a single, circular entrance. The walls were smooth and featureless, save for a few runes etched in the stone by an inset shelf where a bank of candles flickered. Unlike the old shaman's sleeping chamber, there was no clutter of potions and charms. Just a single, broad cushion in the center of the room.

A cushion? Was Gorgul mocking me? The soldiers in my old barracks would have jeered, asking if this was a space for a shaman or a woman recovering from labor. But I stole a glance and saw the guard was still at his station looking perfectly serious.

Even so, I gave the cushion a wide berth.

The only adornment in the room was an old tapestry covering the far wall. The woolen threads were frayed, and their dyes so faded that the designs were hard to discern. The hand-shaped pattern around the border, for instance, was probably red once. But now the threads had turned a murky brown.

I took a few steps back and squinted.

Thanks to the damage time had wrought on the threads, the imagery was confusing and difficult to make out. Eventually, I picked out a single central figure in the tapestry. An orc. The green dye had held up well. On either side of him was a muddled grayish (or maybe whitish) figure, each one smaller than the orc. Similar tapestries hung in my father's hall, so I understood that the scale of the figures was not meant to be literal. The leader was large, while his supporters were smaller–and his enemies smaller still. I was trying to puzzle out if there was another figure behind the orc, or if he really had three arms, when Gorgul warned from the hallway, "Be careful with that—it's a very old relic. Best not give it any reason to disintegrate."

I scanned the room. Had it truly served to provide the clan's shamans with vision? Or was it simply somewhere private to work out exactly what visions they'd claim to have seen?

Since I didn't want the guard to know that I had no idea

how to use the meditation cushion, I rolled the large circle of stone across the doorway and sealed myself away from him. It was a relief...for a few minutes. And then I realized that if I stood there for any amount of time I'd slowly go mad.

I paced the length of the chamber, back and forth, wondering how long exactly a shaman would meditate. Did a series of calisthenics as quietly as possible. And talked myself out of throwing open the door wide simply for the sake of having something to do.

I was just about to start a conversation with the cushion when the sound of stone on stone jerked me to attention and the door rolled aside, revealing Archie.

Back in the sleeping chamber, I could smell someone coming. But the meditation room was so closed off that when the door opened, the scent of human hit me like the flat of a sword. His sweat had an intriguing sharpness to it that was distinctly un-orclike, and it was laced with the copper tang of blood. Immediately, I spotted a large abrasion on his arm, vivid against his pale skin. On an orc, the injury would have blended in, had it even drawn blood at all.

Did he have any concept of how fragile he was? He certainly didn't act like it. Kof was stationed at the door now, and Archie strode right past him, bold as you please. He set a tray of food on the meditation cushion, then broke the silence with a soft murmur, "I've brought your lunch... Droko the Sage."

"If the slave is disturbing you—" Kof began.

"He's not." I considered the guard. The food. The human. "Leave us and seal the door."

As the door rolled shut, I cast back on all the years I'd been trained to do exactly what the guard captain had done—to obey—and what a burden it was to be expected to take the initiative.

The tray was covered with a dome of beaten copper. Archie pulled it off with a flourish and said, "The esteemed chef has prepared an exquisite stew of the choicest dirt-covered root vegetables and the legs of a truly impressive toad. I think there may even be a succulent grub or two."

"You think? Or you know? You said you were the chef."

Archie lifted one shoulder in a playful shrug. "I thought they were some kind of dumplings...till I noticed they were moving. You'll excuse me if I leave those bits for you. I suspect they wouldn't agree with me."

"Fine. Any poison in them would have leached into the sauce by now anyhow."

Archie cocked an eyebrow as he dragged a spoon through the stew, capturing various bits. "At some point, you'll have to trust that I've got no reason to poison you...." He made a show of sliding the spoon into his mouth, then licking it clean...which ended with a wince. "Unfortunately, now that I've used up the ingredients I recognize, I can't really guarantee my results will be palatable."

"Forget about the taste. We're surrounded by scores of herbs and tinctures. Everywhere you turn, there's a bundle of dried leaves or a bowl of pounded roots—any of which could be deadly. Do you know how easy it would be to slip one of them into my food?"

"But we're both newcomers here, strangers to the clan. What reason could I possibly have to want you dead?"

I had no idea how the mind of a human worked. For all I knew, he could taint my food for the sheer enjoyment of watching me squirm. Though the way his sky-colored eyes lingered on me, I realized he could make me squirm plenty with nothing more than a look.

I grabbed the spoon from him and focused on my meal.

I think Archie expected me to speak, but I've never been one for idle chatter. When the silence grew too thick for him to endure, he said, "I can't say I've ever had the pleasure of keeping company with someone important enough to need a food taster—and while I appreciate the job security, I hope you realize that I could be put to much more *creative* uses."

I glanced up from the stew. As I ate, he'd crept closer. Quiet, and soft. His skin was the color of the inner bark of a tree, and looked just as smooth and tender. And his pale neck was so vulnerable I could surely snap it with one hand... though what I really wanted was to press my snout against his warmth and fill myself with its scent.

Something only a babe does at his mother's breast—or a man with his wife.

The image of Farya with my elder brother came to mind, unbidden, and I turned back to my food.

Out of the corner of my eye, I saw Archie smile. "You misunderstand my suggestion, Droko the Sage. Oh, no doubt you'd enjoy putting me through my paces—and I'd surely revel in exploring exactly how different from mine your orcish hotspots and turn-ons may be. But while I am quite skilled in the art of pleasing a man—albeit not through his stomach—what I'm suggesting at this moment is a bit more pragmatic."

His mouth said no—in many more words than it needed—but his teasing eyes told another story. They held my gaze as his delicate human hands dropped to his breeches and his nimble fingers toyed at the waistband.

Had I actually thought the room was too isolated? It hardly seemed that way now. If fact, it struck me as the perfect place to see if the human was anywhere near as pliant as he claimed to be....

But instead of unfastening the ties, he slipped his fingers into a hidden pocket. "I look at things with a different perspective than anyone else who answers to you. All the guards underestimate me—which I suspect might come in handy." He drew out a tightly-rolled slip of parchment. "I'm surprisingly resourceful, see? You ask—and I deliver."

He held onto the scroll more firmly than I expected, which forced our fingertips to brush together as I took it. That meager bit of contact was enough to tease me with how his human skin might feel...but when I opened the scroll, I couldn't make heads or tails of it. The thing was covered in inscrutable symbols.

"What is this supposed to be?" I demanded.

Archie was taken aback. "You're the shaman—I thought you'd have 'eyes to see'!"

The scroll curled over my hand, determined to roll itself up again. I spread it with my fingers and scanned the markings. The leadpoint figures were not proper letters, only a series of hatches and dots, almost like someone had used the parchment to clean up metal filings that had left their impression on the hide. I slapped the scroll down onto the meditation cushion and held it mostly open. "Are you saying you can't read it?" I asked Archie.

The human's cheeks went pink, as did the tips of his ears. "It's not like any kind of writing I've ever seen. I just figured it was how orcs wrote."

I let go with a sigh. The scroll snapped shut. "Orcs write

the same as humans do. Just without all those useless little squiggles and swoops."

"Well, damn." Archie planted his hands on his hips and scowled at the scroll. "I'd been looking forward to your gratitude all day."

Did all humans take failure so lightly? Had I ever delivered such a disappointment to my garrison commander, he would've had me whipped. Probably. If I weren't the chieftain's son, anyhow. "A slave should not expect gratitude." The words were hardly convincing, as mostly I was considering the cant of his hip. My voice sounded thick.

And Archie heard it, too. His eyes twinkled. "Expectation and anticipation are two entirely different things." He dragged a finger through the traces of stew in the bowl and sucked the tip, never dropping my gaze. When I didn't break eye contact, he smiled around his finger—wicked, and full of promise—and eased forward with a suggestive sway of the hips.

But before either of us could take the conversation any further, we were interrupted by a sharp knock. I flinched back as Kof called through the stone door that the chieftain was here. I glanced at Archie as the door rolled open, but now all trace of mischief was gone from his eyes. An undisguised look of nervousness passed between us as we prepared to face Ul-Rott.

10

ARCHIE

In all my time here in the shaman's cave of the Red Hand Clan, Ul-Rott the Spinecrusher had never taken it upon himself to darken the doorstep. Not while I was conscious, anyhow. Not even once Taruut's honor guard finally discovered the ancient shaman had breathed his last mysterious prophecy.

Droko still had two more days to find the crypt. But orcs didn't strike me as being particularly patient, and I wouldn't be surprised to learn the chieftain had come to step up the pace.

We found Ul-Rott and his entourage at the entrance of the cave system, where the cavern was cluttered with carvings and bones, statues and trinkets. I refrained from mentioning the fact that it looked like a stall in a two-bit bazaar that specialized in selling novelties to superstitious tourists. I was smart enough to know when a bit of levity would go over well...but also when I was better off keeping my mouth shut.

As the honor guard stooped and groveled, Ul-Rott took in the chamber with a look of cool assessment. While I'd presumed I didn't much care about whatever it was the orcs found so impressive, when I took stock of Ul-Rott...I realized that notion might not be entirely true. Certainly, there were bigger orcs in the room, and they were decked out in heavier armor and carrying much larger swords. But the chieftain had a magnetism—a *presence*—that no amount of weaponry could replace.

His face was craggy and his eyes were sharp. Strong brow, strong jaw, strong everything. His skin was the muted green of old moss, with a speckling of pebble-colored flecks scattered across his cheekbones. His hair was the greyed black of a tarnished blade, pulled back in a wiry tail. And the chains around his broad neck, forged in gold, were heavy enough to sink a small ship.

Ul-Rott took stock of the room as if the tourist trap ambiance wasn't lost on him, and said, "So. Is this where you work your healing magic?"

He'd said the last few words as if they were patently ridiculous. Droko didn't rise to the bait. In fact, he just narrowed his eyes at the chieftain's skepticism, and the tension in the room went thick.

Either he was baiting the chieftain...or he truly didn't know better than to suggest treating someone in the entryway.

"Forgive me, Droko the Sage," I groveled like a well-trained slave, "but I haven't finished clearing out the *infirmary* yet—I didn't realize we'd be receiving such an esteemed visitor."

The chieftain's gaze skimmed over me, and he spoke to Droko as if I had no more mind than one of the dozens of bird skulls rattling around. "Humans. Strange little things. But surprisingly useful...once you train them up."

But then I realized he wasn't referring to me—at least not

entirely—but another human standing there in the pack, a head shorter than the musclebound orcish guards. The man was all in leather—an elaborate, strappy affair with a whip hanging from the belt—and around his neck was a gold chain nearly as heavy as the chieftain's. His hair hung to his shoulders in glossy, dark waves, and a short goatee framed lips just this side of pretty. But it was his expression that struck me most of all, the look of fierce intensity he was giving me, as if he was trying to get my attention without the orcs being any the wiser....

I'll be damned. The guy in the fancy leather was Quinn. Well...didn't *he* clean up nice?

But now wasn't the time for reunions.

Ul-Rott shifted his shoulders uneasily and said, "Let's get this over with. I'm none too fond of skulking around inside the earth like a bunch of goblins—unnatural, if you ask me. No light. No breeze. And it stinks like a clutch of eggs forgotten in the larder. Lead the way, Archie."

I started as he said my name.

My shock seemed to amuse the chieftain. "Yes, I'm fully aware of who you are. Taruut may have been living in his own little world—but he was still my shaman, and when he spoke, I heard him." He waved a dismissive hand at the guards—both his and the shaman's alike. "You stay here. I don't want you breathing up all my air."

"And me?" Quinn addressed the chieftain directly, bold as you please. Still as arrogant as ever. "Should I stay?"

"You, come along. You might prove useful."

Gorgul was looking at the chieftain expectantly, like he was hoping to be singled out as well. And I imagine he was especially annoyed with me when it didn't happen.

I was glad enough to leave him and all the rest of the guards behind. The entrance of the cave system was grand, but the tunnels quickly narrowed. And there was only one orc I had any desire to brush up against.

I led the group down the warren of paths that opened into the sauna chamber where I'd spent so much time recuperating on my hard, stony bed. While I wouldn't say it felt like home, exactly, it was most definitely familiar. The stone surfaces had been hewn with care to integrate harmoniously with the natural formations in the chamber. Mist gave the room a hazy ambience, and the humid air was soothing to my lungs...even if it did, indeed, smell like rotten eggs.

The last time I saw Quinn, he was in rags—and I was flat on my back, drifting in and out of consciousness. I was absolutely dying to talk to him again and find out how he'd managed such a striking reversal of fortune, though I hadn't much hope of it happening while the chieftain was in the room. I'll say one thing about orcs: their pecking order is crystal clear.

And then Ul-Rott surprised me by conveniently shooing us aside. "Out of our way, little slaves. I need to consult the shaman."

"You've certainly come up in the world," I murmured as Quinn and I did our best to fade into the background. "That chain around your neck could buy my whole brothel. Maybe my whole village. And here I thought you were far too old to be a bedboy."

I was only teasing—but even by the meager light of the braziers, I could see him blush.

"Well...I'll be. You *are* polishing a big, green rod. Looks like you've made the best out of a bad situation."

"It's not like that."

"—but I guess being the chieftain's concubine does have its perks."

"The—?" Quinn barked out a laugh, which earned him a nervous glance from Droko and a look of annoyance from the chieftain. He lowered his voice and said, "I'm just the chieftain's horseman."

He could protest all he wanted, but I wasn't born yesterday. "Sure, you are." I flicked his gold chain for emphasis. "And I'm a trembling virgin."

"Ul-Rott didn't give me this." He settled his hand over the chain, fingering the heavy links. "Marok did."

A person might argue that you can't read much into the utterance of a few simple words. But it was clear to me that Quinn thought of the dour orc as more than just protection. "What about you?" he asked. "Are you okay?"

"For the time being." Until someone poisoned the pantry, at any rate...or until I killed myself with my own dubious cooking. Quinn, always the cleverest one in the room—at least in his own mind—proceeded to avail me of the wisdom he'd gleaned over his many weeks living among the clan. Everything he told me, I'd figured out just by watching Gargle kowtow to the new shaman, but I didn't bother to mention it. I was preoccupied with figuring out Droko's body language as he spoke in low tones with the chieftain. Droko had fallen into his especially stiff and formal mode... the one he used when he was backed into a corner.

Ul-Rott seemed to make a big point of respecting his shaman. In fact, after the chieftain, the shaman was the most powerful member of the clan.

So, why was Droko nervous?

I shushed Quinn so I could eavesdrop on the orcs' conversation.

"Of course, I'd normally have the shaman come to me," Ul-Rott was saying. "The weight of all this rock pressing down on your head, the hiss of the steam, the sound of constant dripping...it's no wonder Taruut was so batty. But a chieftain can't show weakness in front of his clan."

"And we don't qualify as men, you and I," Quinn whispered. "More like glorified lap dogs."

I was about to tell him to speak for himself...but my thoughts went blank as the chieftain unhitched his belt and let his breeches fall to his knees...and his mammoth dick flopped out.

Dang. If he could train that thing to hold a sword, he'd be unstoppable.

"I've been too busy dealing with your former clan lately to have any time for coupling," he told Droko...who'd gone even *more* still. "So, give it to me straight. Has that whoreson across the river managed to lay a curse on me? Or did my wife pick up something from one of her ogres that's been festering beneath my skin for months, only to erupt at the worst possible moment? I'm sure you've heard stories about Destroyer. Well, believe me when I say that riding that beast is nowhere near as effortless as I make it look. And now I'm plagued with some kind of pox right where I need it the least."

I couldn't tear my eyes away from the monstrous green dick, but Quinn was apparently inured to such daunting sights. "It's no pox," he whispered. "All that chafing in the crooks of his thighs—those are saddlesores."

In true Quinn fashion, he was about to pipe up and proclaim his vast knowledge to the room, just in case they didn't already realize how smart he thought he was. "Wait," I told him. "Let Droko do the talking."

Droko considered the chieftain, then stepped forward and made several cryptic gestures. He murmured a few unrecognizable words as he rubbed his hands together and cupped them over Ul-Rott's exposed groin. Once he was satisfied with whatever he'd gleaned from his "examination," he straightened up and declared, "The shaman of the Two Swords Clan doesn't have the strength to curse you at such a distance."

"Are you sure? I paraded back and forth across that new river fjord at least half a dozen times...."

"While the shaman cowered in his hut."

People claim a fish hasn't a clue that water's wet—but Droko knew just what to say. Of course, I wasn't actually *worried* about him—me, a mere human, and him a powerful shaman who obviously had everything figured out—

"But ogres *can* carry a certain taint...."

Though only in terms of telling Ul-Rott what he wanted to hear!

Before Droko gave the chieftain something that would only make his malady worse, I hurried over to Taruut's collection of herbs and unguents. I grabbed a pot of ointment he'd used to soothe the abrasions the rough metal slave collar had left on my neck. "A thousand apologies, my shaman," I told Droko, "but I moved things around while I was organizing."

I shoved the small ceramic jar into his hand, and he met my gaze...and held it. Just for the fraction of a heartbeat, but that was plenty. If I wanted to sabotage Droko, this would be the perfect way. Did he trust me enough to treat his chieftain?

He gave the concoction a sniff, tested it between his fingers, then handed it over to Ul-Rott. "The slave is still learning."

Ul-Rott side-eyed the salve. "Seems like more trouble than he's worth—but Taruut was fond of him, so maybe he's got some potential." He hitched up his pants and turned toward the exit. It seemed the harrowing exchange was nearly over—and somehow, we'd passed muster.

And then, of course, the chieftain had to go and ruin it by adding, "I'll bet you'd snap that boy like a twig. Good thing your vows forbid you to couple."

11

DROKO

Once Ul-Rott took his leave, I dismissed the guards, reminding them that we only had two days to find the crypt. And thanks to the chieftain's lengthy visit, time was running out fast.

After the orcs cleared out, the only ones left were me...and Archie. The human who'd just saved my hide—or, at the very least, helped me look like a plausible shaman. Which probably amounted to the same thing.

But before I could acknowledge his service, he gave me a cool look and said, "If that will be all, Droko the Sage." He knelt briefly, tapping one knee on the cave floor. "It's been a very long night."

I've always found the expressions of creatures without tusks fairly difficult to read. But the grim line of Archie's mouth made it abundantly clear that he was none too thrilled. Without even waiting for my dismissal, he turned on his heel and walked off into the mist.

But I soon realized I wasn't alone. Gorgul strode into the chamber and presented himself with a deep genuflection.

"Droko the Sage, my spear is yours."

The honorifics were starting to get tedious. Or maybe it was the way Archie had said the title, cold and inflectionless, that was burrowing under my skin. "What is it?" I asked the lieutenant...when what I wanted to say was, *What is it now?*

"My shaman...the men have been scouring the caves all day and night, and they are no closer to finding the crypt than they were when you arrived." While there was no reproach in Gorgul's voice, it was clear he thought we had a problem. "If the slaves are too distracting, I can take them off your hands—"

Without the slaves—without *Archie*—I would have pronounced the chieftain cursed and sent him on his way. But obviously, I could never let Gorgul suspect. "Tell me, Gorgul. How long have you lived in these caves?"

The question surprised him. "Many years. More than I have ever stopped to count."

"Then, why would I waste your time with slaves when I need your expertise to find the crypt?"

"I'm honored by your confidence," he said. I sensed a "but" coming. "But the caves are treacherous and several of the passages are unexplored. If the way forward is unclear, is it not the task of the shaman to divine the best path? And how can he do so if he's distracted by slaves—?"

"Enough," I said. I needed counsel, but he took too many liberties. "I don't need an honor guard to defend me within my own walls. You will take all the men, break into teams, and scour these tunnels until you find the crypt. Understood?"

"My shaman is wise," Gorgul murmured, genuflecting yet again.

I bit back a sigh. I was thinking like a soldier flushing out an enemy, not a shaman. And so, before he rose to leave, I added, "Meanwhile, I will toss the ivories and see what I can divine."

That seemed to please the guard. He bobbed another half-bow as he backed out the door.

As much as I liked having good men to do my bidding, it was a relief to be alone...a relief that was short-lived. Once Gorgul's footsteps faded, a familiar, ugly gray figure emerged from the mists, clapping mockingly. "Tossing the ivories?" Crespash said. "This oughtta be good."

When a young boy shows the signs that will mark him as a future acolyte, his parents save his milk teeth as they shed instead of sacrificing them on the family hearth. These teeth are the prize possession of any shaman, more valuable than gold. Most orcs will never witness a shaman consulting his precious sack of teeth. But I was the son of a chieftain, and I vividly recalled watching from my sleeping loft as the shaman cast his teeth right on the grand table of my father's hall. The audible clatter they made against the wood sent a chill creeping down my neck—a chill that still shivered through me, to this day, whenever I thought about that visit.

I, of course, had no spare teeth.

Unlike orcs, goblins don't shed milk teeth. Their rows of blade-like fangs grow throughout their lives. So, Crespash could have chipped some "ivories" out of his own mouth for me—had his teeth not been prized out at the root long ago...on my father's orders. An irony that was surely not lost on the goblin.

"What's wrong?" he sneered. "Is Droko the Sage not wise enough to deduce some meaning from a handful of rocks?"

"Watch your tongue. Sound carries in these tunnels."

"Oh, and now you're the expert in caves, as well! What other secret talents have you been harboring all these years? Perhaps you're now a master musician. Or a sea captain." He pawed through the herbs, locating a bundle of dried berries that he popped into his mouth, winced, and spat out again. "Too bad you're not a crypt-finder. Because that's the only talent that will keep our heads firmly seated on our necks when Taruut's funeral rolls around."

"You mean to tell me you were searching all night with nothing to show for it?"

"I wouldn't say that," he drawled. Playing coy—or just taunting me? "At any rate, if you plan on seeing another summer, I suggest we go find that damn crypt."

Crespash needed no light, though he didn't grumble over me taking a lantern. Low-hanging fruit, I supposed. We set off to the main hub of the caves, where I found the guard captain Kof scratching a diagram into the floor with a shard of chalk. "I'm keeping track of who's gone where, my shaman."

"Strategy is well and good, but we need every man searching, including you. Pick one of the unexplored tunnels and handle it yourself."

"As my shaman commands." With a grim nod, Kof took up his lantern and lumbered away.

Once he was out of earshot, Crespash said, "There are rumors about that one."

"What rumors?"

"That he lost his eye to some ill luck. And Taruut's favor was the only thing keeping his guards loyal."

"They're soldiers," I said, "and they're orcs. There may be

idle talk, but the guardsmen will stay in line because that's what they've been trained to do."

"If you say so, *wise one*."

Ignoring the jibe, I gazed down at the map chalked onto the floor. "Is it accurate?" I asked.

The goblin shrugged. "Close enough." He ran a finger-stump along a sharply-curved hallway. "This slopes downward, then curves around on itself." He smudged out the path and redrew it with arrows to make it more precise. "And this chamber is a lot smaller." He sketched a line. Considered it. Then drew another shape…the shape of an engorged cock fucking the gap between the chambers.

"Will you be serious?" I snapped.

He added a few hairs to the ballsack. "If the crypt were in any of these obvious places, I would've found it by now. It's been decades since it was last seen. But I suppose it was best to send your guards on a fool's errand before one of them noticed how clueless you are."

"I'll have you know I just cured the chieftain." Thanks to Archie…though I didn't want to give Crespash any reason to be jealous. Goblins are petty things—and humans so incredibly fragile. Even without teeth or claws, Crespash was perfectly capable of tearing the young man to shreds.

"Maybe today you were lucky. But what about tomorrow? All it takes is a big enough mistake for them all to figure out you're a fraud."

"Shamans are known for being cryptic," I said. Crespash rolled his eyes. "I can do this," I insisted. "I have no other choice."

"Don't you? The caves run deep—deeper than I thought—and clearly, the orcs don't know the half of them. They say there's no way out.... But what if you were looking for a tomb and you happened to stumble across an exit?"

"What are you saying—there *is* a way out?"

"Just exploring the possibility."

Goblins. Always wallowing in nonsense. "Even if I could slip away—even if I did manage to evade any soldiers they sent after me...I'd only bring retribution to my clan."

"Your *former* clan. Who married off your woman before you even had a chance to squeeze her tits."

"Even so. There's more than just me to consider. If I break the covenant, the chieftain's family will bear the brunt of my failure. My mother, my sisters...how would I live with myself if I fled like a coward and they were the ones who got punished?"

As I rubbed out the grotesque penis drawing with the sole of my boot, Crespash gave a humorless laugh. "Why not save yourself? Surely, at some point, the charade will come undone."

"A general can establish his career on one good win. The same does hold true for a shaman."

"Once we find the crypt, I suppose you could swap out your bag of pebbles for the dead orc's milk teeth," Crespash said. "Still, a single cure does not a shaman make."

If he'd seen the afflicted area, he might reconsider exactly how grateful Ul-Rott would be. "I can learn. Archie has some skill with healing. He can teach me—"

"You'd put your very life in the hands of a slave?" Crespash snorted. "Then you're even dumber than I thought."

12

ARCHIE

Never get attached.

It's the cardinal rule of a working boy. Sure, you have your regulars. But the day always comes when they show up at the red lantern with coin in their pocket and a bulge in their pants...and they beckon you over...only to ask if there's anyone new.

The bedboys who pout about it—or even throw a hissy fit—are the ones who guarantee they'll never win back their old clientele. So the fact that there is no happily-ever-after for someone like me...well, I've learned to grin and bear it.

So what if I couldn't hope to bed the hot young shaman? I'd prove myself useful in other ways. After all, it wasn't as if I'd ever *aspired* to being a prostitute. It was just the hand I'd been dealt by fate.

As I slipped down the winding tunnel, I tried to imagine myself as something else. Something more. A confidante. An advisor.

And yet, all those imaginings somehow managed to culminate in me tugging open the ties on the shaman's leathers and watching them slither to the floor. I'd always prided myself on having a good imagination. But this was one instance where I would be better off without it.

The sound of my footfalls changed as the passage opened out to a larger cavern, and my lantern beam was swallowed by the opening. Judging by the undisturbed grit beneath my soles, no one had come this way in a long time. Which would make it an ideal place to lick my wounds in peace....

Or maybe not. The chamber was good-sized, but cluttered, and hard to see by a single light. I opened my lantern and held it high, and shadows danced wildly.

It was a storeroom—or it had been, once. But the shelves were swathed in something I took for fabric, initially. Until I realized I was looking at sheaves of webbing and the collapsed shapes of cocoons. And that the grit crunching under my feet was made up of the crumbling shells of some kind of insect.

My initial instinct was to run. But it was obvious that whatever was once breeding here had long ago dried up. I found a shard of rock and used it to clear away some of the webbing. It was thicker than I expected, but brittle, too, and it parted with ease. Small carcasses filled the shelves in drifts. Spiders. Some normal-sized, some as big as my hand. Thankfully, all long-dead. But once I got beyond the creepy, eight-legged confetti, I saw the shelves had once held something other than bugs. Vessels of wood or clay or glass. It was like Taruut's stash of tinctures and herbs, but enough to supply an army.

I uncorked a stoneware jar and tipped out a sifting of dust. Whatever army this storehouse might have served was long dead, and the shaman who'd amassed it was already moldering in the mysterious hidden crypt.

The herbs were useless, but that didn't mean there was nothing here I could use. I dragged a brazier closer to the shelves. The wood inside was beyond desiccated, and when I coaxed flame into it from my lantern, it blazed to life with a startling crackle.

The light illuminated even more crunchy mounds of spider bodies—ew—but up above, on the highest shelf...was that a scroll case? Maybe there really was a map after all! Since the shelving was built for orcs, I couldn't quite tell what I'd found from where I stood. But I'm not a bad climber, and if I cleared away enough of the spiders....

"Well—look who's here."

I jumped and whirled around, only to find Gorgul standing in one of the doorways with his hand resting on his spear. His footsteps must've been camouflaged by the crackling of the old wood! Still, there were even more guards behind him, and I should have heard them coming. I *would* have... if I hadn't been so focused on the scrolls.

Gorgul handed off his lantern to an underling and strode into the chamber, making no attempt now to tread softly. His steps were punctuated by alarming crunches. "Weak little humans should take care in snooping around unfamiliar caves." He picked up a skeletal carcass the size of a sea crab. "If this cave spider were still alive, she'd eat her way through your soft belly and pump you full of eggs. And you can see how eagerly they breed."

He tossed the dried spider in my direction. I dodged, and it shattered against a dusty shelf.

"You're not nearly as clever as you believe," he went on, scanning the room. "What is it you think you've found?

There's nothing here anyone would care about. Nothing here but rot and ruin. Face it, human. There's only one thing a whore like you can offer—and it's nothing that would interest a shaman."

I'd quit being ashamed of my profession years ago. And yet, somehow, the orc's insult cut me to the bone. Probably because it came on the heels of me entertaining the notion that I could ingratiate myself to Droko. Because it hit me right where a sliver of hope had breached my heart.

I knew damn well that hope is for suckers. But it stung nonetheless.

The worst part was, that horrible guard could tell he'd gotten to me. A grin of smug satisfaction curled around his tusks as he basked in my humiliation. He'd be singing a different tune, though, once I brought that scroll to Droko.

His gaze followed mine and landed on the cracked leather case. Without so much as straining, he plucked it from the high shelf and my heart sank. Now he'd be the hero...and I'd be just another puny slave.

"There's nothing here," Gorgul repeated...and dropped the scroll case onto the flaming brazier.

The leather case might have protected it, once. But not now. Hungry flames chewed through the cracked leather sheath as I watched my one chance at impressing the new shaman go up in smoke.

Gorgul took a step in my direction. I'm sure he would've loved nothing more than to grab me by the hair and shove my face into the smoking coals.

The long knife hidden in my trousers weighed against my thigh, but it was obvious he'd spear me before I got close enough to use it. Still, my sense of self-preservation is finely honed, and before he could catch me, I'd grabbed my lantern and slipped through a crack between two shelves that was too narrow for him to follow.

"Go, little human," he called after me. "Scatter like the vermin you are. You can't hide forever. Eventually you'll end up like the spiders. Dried up and dead."

Not gonna lie...I may have broken into a nervous sweat. It turned out to be an asset for slipping through a particularly punishing gap. Gorgul wasn't wrong. If I got lost in the stony labyrinth, there was only so long I could last without food or drink. But, who knows? Maybe, by that time, I would grow thin enough to shove myself through a gap that led to freedom.

Unfortunately, it was just as likely I'd only find myself wandering deeper into the earth. I squeezed out into yet another stony chamber, about as big around as the parlor of a fancy brothel. My sense of direction seemed fine back in Wildwood, where I never got lost, even when a new crop of lean-tos sprang up where mere days before, there'd been a road. But the caves, carved by the capriciousness of water, followed their own flowing paths that were nothing like the constructs of men.

And even worse...after a while, they all looked the same. Same rugged walls. Same threatening stalactites.

Same crescent-shaped gap.

I'd circled back around to the sword! I crammed through the gap and fumbled into the crevice where it was hidden, panicking momentarily as my grasp closed on thin air. But then my fingertips brushed the smooth pommel, and I swayed with relief as I drew out the sword.

I imagined that dumb oaf Gargle coming at me with a

spear, only for it to shear right in half as I raised my glorious blade. That was supposing I was able to lift it in time—which, honestly, would be a stretch. But a guy can always dream.

Of course, it would be even more satisfying to cleave Gorgul in two like I'd sliced through the stone bier. But, setting aside that I didn't have the strength...if I somehow did manage, the memory would undoubtedly haunt me for the rest of my days.

I dragged the sword from its hiding place and reacquainted myself with the shape of the hilt. My fantasies about becoming the shaman's confidante were no better than the spider carcasses. Dust and ruin. If Droko let me serve him, it would never be as anything other than a slave. And Gorgul would make sure that my time in service was as short as possible. In other words...there was nothing for me here.

I had to go.

I shoved through to the chamber where the stumpy figures lay in petrified eternal rest—not because I thought they could help me, but because it was the last place I'd seen the sky. My eyes were accustomed to the low light of the lantern, but outside, it was daylight now. The light beaming through the shaft a dozen feet overhead made my eyes water, and I squinted as I adjusted to the brightness.

I didn't know exactly where that shaft would lead, but the only sound filtering down was the rustle of wind through branches and the chatter of an annoyed bluejay. Not the sort of sounds you'd hear within the walls of an orcish village.

I pressed the tip of the sword into the cavern floor. There was resistance.... And then it pushed through as if the floor were clay, not stone. I might not be able to reach that shaft in the center of the ceiling without a grappling hook. But if I carved steps into the stone wall and reached the ceiling, maybe I could tunnel my own way out.

A circuit of the chamber revealed a craggy diagonal ridge that almost read as a stairway—if you looked at it just right and squinted hard enough. Parts of it were too narrow to even qualify as a toehold, and stretches of it were nearly vertical. But as I hacked off a shard of stone with my preternaturally sharp blade, I saw that with a bit of help, stairs could emerge.

It was slow work. I found a rhythm with the tool, getting a feel for the best angle to hold the blade and exactly how much stone I could hew away with a single stroke. But even as I got the hang of it, my shoulders began to ache and my arms trembled with fatigue.

By the time I could no longer lift the heavy sword, I'd carved all of three steps. Steep, narrow, precarious things barely the width of my foot.

Good thing I'd only need to use them once.

My stomach growled, and I stashed my sword in its niche to head for the kitchen before anyone wondered where I'd gone. Gorgul would probably think I'd been hiding from him, and that was fine by me. People tended to underestimate me. Might as well use it to my advantage.

The gnarly old cook at the brothel always shooed whores out of the kitchen so no one could take more than their fair share of the slop, so I was working by instinct alone. Even worse, I didn't recognize most of the ingredients. At least, I thought I didn't....

Until I unstoppered a jar of reddish seeds and inhaled their intoxicating spice...and recalled Taruut's words.

The berry of the Rubyseed plant is a capricious thing. Harvest them too young, and they'll pucker your mouth. Too old, and you'll shit for days. But at their pinnacle of ripeness, the taste is so exquisite, clans have fought wars for a wagonload of the fruit.

The Rubyseed he'd shown me back then was on the ripe side—a cure for constipation. But the bottle in my hand was clearly of the war-starting variety.

Couldn't care less if Droko likes my cooking, I told myself as I stewed some jerky and dried roots, and seasoned them with the rare spice. *Just making myself seem useful so I don't end up in the slave pits before I cut my way out of here.*

13

DROKO

One by one, my teams of explorers returned to report all the passageways in which they didn't find the crypt. And one by one, I chalked their routes onto the floor. As the day wore on, the map tripled in size.

And still...no crypt.

Kof stood beside me, glaring down at the map. His shoulders drooped. But he made no move to stop searching. "We must have missed something. I'll go back and check again."

A good general knows when to march his troops, and when to rest.

"Go back to your barracks," I told him. "We'll take up the search in the morning. It's been a long day."

"Indeed it has," said a goblin voice, once the guard captain was out of earshot. "But you may want to savor it. There may not be many more ahead of you."

"Are you telling me you *still* haven't found it?"

"Your predecessor lived to a ripe old age...which means the crypts haven't seen any use in our lifetimes. Maybe even our fathers' lifetimes. If there ever was a trail for me to pick up, the years erased it long ago. But I didn't come entirely empty-handed."

He unhitched a pouch from his belt and presented me with a cloth sack.

"It's not a crypt. But it may buy you some time."

There was a round bulge in the sack about the size of a spring melon, but it was lighter than it looked. I opened it and peered inside, and was greeted by the bony curve of a skull. "What am I supposed to do with this?"

Crespash sighed and rolled his oversized eyes. "You need ivories? Take this poor sod's—he won't be needing them."

I turned the skull in its swaddling of burlap and inspected the teeth. Only a few were missing.

"Good," I said brusquely.

It was probably the highest praise I'd ever given the goblin...and he noticed. "You're not in the clear just yet. You've still got a chieftain breathing down your neck and a crypt to find. And only one more day in which to do it."

"We'll find it. I have a whole team of guards searching."

"Maybe so. But who's to say they're actually looking? Trust no one, and you won't be disappointed." Crespash sidled toward one of the tunnels, readying himself to slip off into the warren of passageways. "No one."

This was the way goblins thought. Always scrambling for power, always willing to step on whoever it took to get it. He didn't understand that orcs knew the strength of the clan was more important than personal glory. Yes, the one who found the crypt would hope to be acknowledged. But there was no doubt in my mind that they were all looking.

I thrust a hand into the sack and pried at an incisor, but soon realized I'd need to get a good look at what I was doing, or else risk ruining the teeth. But not here.

I headed to the only spot I knew I'd be undisturbed: the meditation chamber. I rolled the stone into place, relieved to finally be safe from prying eyes. My guards might be loyal—but if they found out I was no shaman, the natural order of things would be shattered.

As I lit the brazier from a torch I carried, the room danced with firelight, and the old tapestry fluttered. Back when Gorgul had first offered me the room, it had felt too close, too quiet. But now that I was more familiar with the space, I felt a calmness steal over me. Probably just relief at being able to pull some teeth without anyone seeing. But it was a welcome change.

I squatted beside the ludicrous cushion and pulled out my eating knife. I kept the blade keen and the point sharp, and soon I'd managed to pry out a good handful of ivory.

The teeth were definitely better than pebbles, but I wasn't sure they'd pass muster if anyone looked at them too hard. They seemed awfully large. What I needed was a child's skull.

Or a human's.

A tap on the round stone door snapped me to attention. "It's suppertime, Droko the Sage," called Archie. "Don't make me set down this tray to open the door—evidently, you might end up with spider babies in your food. Though maybe orcs are into that sort of thing...."

I swept the teeth into my belt pouch and tucked the skull behind the hem of the tapestry, then rolled the heavy stone door aside.

The human stood there in the doorway in his linens, with a platter in his hands and a challenge in his eyes. But it wasn't the way he looked that struck me. It was the way he smelled—like human sweat.

Sharp. Pungent.

Good.

The last time I'd been this close to him—that morning, when he'd slipped me the cure for the chieftain's ailment—he'd smelled of human, certainly. But also of sulfur and herbs. Now, though, the scent of him filled my nostrils, alluring and rich—laced with something else I couldn't quite place.

I parted my lips and let the scent settle on my palate. It played across the back of my tongue like a mystery.

"I knew you'd be hungry," he said, and shouldered his way into the room.

He plunked the tray on the meditation cushion. Sacrilege, no doubt. But no worse than me using it to pry out a dead man's teeth.

"Are we still playing the little game where you pretend I'm going to poison you?" he asked breezily. "Not that I mind, of course. I think I'm getting the hang of orcish cuisine."

He plucked the dome off the food, and the smell of the meal blotted out everything else. Not the venison. And not the cave carrots.

But the spice.

Rubyseed was as rare as the gemstone it was named for—so rare it was reserved only for special occasions. Like birthdays. And victory feasts.

And weddings.

There's a cask of rubyseed as big as your footlocker waiting for your wedding day. Farya will never forget how lucky she is to be part of the Two Swords Clan.

My father had been so proud. Not to celebrate my wedding—the wedding that never happened. But to make a show of dominance after his crushing defeat by Ul-Rott.

Archie took a spoonful and smacked his lips. "Maybe it's an acquired...taste."

He trailed off when I covered the ground between us in two strides, stopping short just shy of pressing myself against him. The scent of human mingled with the smell of Ruby-seed. It was intoxicating.

He looked up, his eyes wide.

"What?" he asked cautiously.

I didn't answer–I couldn't. I just stood there, lost in the scent.

Then his eyes narrowed and he fell back a step. "Having fun?"

"What do you mean?" I demanded.

"This little game you're playing—tease the lowly human."

"I don't know what you're talking about."

"Truly, I can't imagine why I care," he said with false breeziness. "And no doubt it's amusing, you puffing up all big and virile whenever we're close. Gazing at me like you're undressing me with your eyes. Lavishing looks upon me brimming with promise...knowing full well you've no intention of making good on them."

The urge to grab him and drag him up against me—to bury my nose in the crook of his slender neck—was over-whelming. "You have no idea what I intend."

"Is that so? What about your vow of celibacy?"

"I took no vow." The words came out low and rough. I risked everything by telling him that—and I knew that trust-ing him might be my undoing. But I couldn't help myself.

The sardonic smile froze on his face, coloring with some-thing part hope, part fear. "Truly?" he said, so softly it was barely a breath. "No wonder you seem so hesitant about all this shaman business. You're no acolyte." He smiled knowingly as I sucked in a gasp. If the human knew me for a soldier, it was only a matter of time before the honor guard caught on.

Archie smiled wider. "You're a novice, at best."

Relief flooded me as I closed the small gap between us and dipped down to bathe in his scent....

And then stopped myself, knowing that if the other orcs smelled him on me, Archie's head would end up on a stake—right beside mine.

As I backed off, Archie's eyes went cold. "Hah—you almost had me going there. I actually thought you wanted me—"

I grabbed him by the arm before he could turn away and gave him a rough shake. "What I want makes no difference. If I lay with you, the others will know."

"They certainly wouldn't hear about it from me!"

"It makes no difference. My scent mingled with yours would damn us faster than any accusation possibly could."

A sly understanding dawned in Archie's eyes. "Well, if the pesky little matter of life and death is all that's holding you back...." He smiled a secret smile. "I pride myself in being *very* creative."

My heart beat so loud I was sure he could hear it. "What are you saying?"

He glanced down at my hand clenched around his upper arm. "I can get big results from a surprisingly small point of contact. A long time ago, I figured out that the power of seduction isn't about a tight ass or a practiced stroke. It's about the mind."

My hand dropped to my side...but I stood my ground. Even when Archie's eyes raked me up and down, and his scent shifted, growing even headier. This thing we played at could get us both killed. But desire surged within me so sudden and fierce that the risk paled in the light of my need.

As a soldier, I'd been prepared for many things. I drilled to take on an opponent with a sword or a spear. I practiced anticipating an enemy's move. I even learned to fend off an attack from all sides. But this burning ache consuming me from the inside out was something I'd never experienced before. And I hadn't the first idea how to fight it.

Only that the urge must be slaked.

"You're wearing wa-a-ay too many clothes," Archie purred. "Take off those leathers."

I unhitched my cloak and fumbled at my armor's lacings with fingers that somehow managed to be both over-sensitized and numb. It was madness to let a slave give me orders—yet I was powerless against his command. It should have been ridiculous, him in his children's linens.

It was anything but.

I lifted my chest piece over my head, and Archie's eyes roamed my body. "So chiseled I can see…. Every. Last. Muscle."

Surely, now, he'd know me for the soldier I was. No acolyte would be so fit.

But that wasn't the conclusion Archie had drawn. "I'll bet you feel amazing. Skim your fingertips down your chest. Slowly. That's me—learning you with my fingers and tongue. Exploring every hill and valley. Every rock-hard inch."

The touch of my own hand was hardly anything to get excited about. But with Archie watching, sensation lit my body as I trailed my fingers down my chest. He reached down and adjusted himself and the scent of human arousal flooded my senses.

"I promise you this, shaman...someday, that touch truly will be mine. Once you've made your mark in this clan—once no one would ever think to question you—we'll figure out exactly how to cover our tracks. Between the geyser and the herbs, there's gotta be a way." His gaze dropped to the lacings on my breeches. "And when we find it...."

He folded to his knees, and my entire world narrowed to the dart of his small pink tongue on his lower lip...and the thrumming of my pulse in my painfully-stiff cock.

"When we finally find it...I'll do things to you that you've never even imagined."

No doubt. He already was.

"Show me," he said, urgent and low. "Show me the hulking beast that's straining to bust out."

I thought it would be a relief to free my aching cock, but when I pulled it out, the sight of it bobbing there inches from Archie's upturned face only made its need grow sharper. "Touch it," he whispered. "With *my* hand. It's so big and meaty I can't even close my fist around it. But I don't let that stop me."

My breath caught as familiar calluses rasped against my shaft. Surely, it felt nothing like Archie's nimble, smooth human hand. But I was too far gone now to care.

"Damn. That head's like a fist. And the veins...never in my life have I seen such girth. And it makes my mouth water."

"Tell me," I grunted, pumping my shaft. My balls drew up and arousal clenched my body. I wanted to take him and use him, and make him cry out and spurt his hot human seed.

"So big. And I'll bet you taste divine...."

Archie's eyelids closed as he swayed forward, cheeks flushed, utterly fuckable. His hot breath played across the gleaming tautness of my cockhead, and from that alone—a mere whisper of sensation—I found myself spiraling toward the point of no return.

Nothing else mattered—not the clan or the crypt or the fact that a sharpened stake was surely waiting for my head. Just the sweet, wet promise of Archie's ripe lips.

The surge ignited somewhere deep in my guts. It flared fast, overtaking all my senses, with the power of a thrown spear. Wetness. The merest trace of a soft, human tongue skimmed my slit—Archie's tongue—and I became the spear. Hurtling toward my target. Relentless. Unstoppable.

Even as I lost control, I scrambled to regain it—but I was too far gone. My thighs trembled as my legs locked, and pleasure roared through me that was just this side of pain. I'd denied myself far too long for a reward that would never come. This would have been my wedding night. And instead of spending myself with my mate, the one I would mark with my scent was this fragile human slave....

Who rolled to one side just as my seed pumped into the empty air where his sweet mouth had been a moment before.

His breathing was rough—almost as rough as mine—as we looked at the evidence of this thing we'd just done, painted across the meditation room floor in pearly strands. We'd barely touched each other, it was true. But a real shaman would never have let things go so far.

And that realization made fear take hold. "They'll know," I said. "The guards will know."

"What?" Archie scoffed. "How?"

"They'll scent it."

"And here I thought Gargle was exaggerating this whole sense-of-smell thing just to get a rise out of me. But worry not, my shaman. I've got this." He pushed to his feet and grabbed the meal he'd prepared—the stew heavy with rare rubyseed—and dumped the entire bowl on the floor, obliterating my spend.

14

ARCHIE

"Whoops," I said innocently as the stew sloshed over Droko's jiz. "Clumsy me. Let me wipe that up."

I peeled off my linen tunic, grateful to be rid of it in the stifling heat of the caves, and swabbed up the mess on the floor before it attracted any of those hideous spiders. "There. All set. Now, I don't know about you, but I'm utterly exhausted." And that big cushion in the middle of the room was the only comfortable surface I'd seen in weeks.

Droko was looking at me like I'd just grown a second head. "But—you—" he stammered.

"I what?"

He made a vague wanking gesture.

Worried about me not getting off? Unexpected. And unexpectedly sweet.

"Don't worry, that'll keep." Most paying men didn't care whether or not I was satisfied, after all. So, I'd had plenty of practice at denying myself.

I curled up on the cushion while the shaman pulled on his leathers and settled on the floor, flat on his back, with his hands folded over his chest. He looked eerily like the petrified men I'd found deep within the caves, the ones with the strange writing and the sharp sword. I considered Droko by the light of the mostly-shuttered lantern, how his strong brow and thick jaw were looking not just familiar to me, but desirable. And I thought about how empowering it was when I made him come utterly undone with nothing but a few filthy ideas and the smallest sweep of my tongue. If there'd been any question as to whether or not he wanted me, that doubt was put firmly to rest.

Eventually, my hard-on ebbed, though the ache of want in my belly lingered. Those things I'd said about finding a way to be together were just words. Something to push the shaman toward the brink. But like any good lie, it held a grain of truth. If the herbs couldn't cover our tracks, a blast from the Great Whale surely would....

Nope. I sighed and rolled onto my back. Not gonna go there. This dalliance could never be more than a quick fling. Inside these caves, Droko might be the head honcho. But even he had rules to follow. Rules he couldn't—or wouldn't—break.

Besides. I was only a few stairsteps away from escape.

And yet....

The noise he'd made deep in his throat. That small, broken sound. I'd done that to such a magnificent creature. Me. And I'd be lying if I said I wasn't eager to try it again. Yes, a few more hacks at the stone wall would let me slip off into the night and find my fortune outside these caves. But I hadn't yet felt the big, strong shaman's arms around me...and surely I couldn't leave without a proper goodbye.

The room was warm and the cushion was soft, and

despite my restless thoughts, I fell into a deep and satisfying slumber—

Only to be woken by the deep rumble of an orcish voice. "No...no...."

Droko's head jerked side to side in his sleep as his eyes darted around beneath closed lids, but the rest of him was locked down tight. Back in Wildwood, when I was between brothels, I once stayed with a guy who *didn't* freeze up while he was dreaming. I took such a battering from his flailing limbs that my friends thought he was beating me. Luckily Droko didn't act out his dreams. If he did, no doubt he could do some serious damage.

"Hey." I reached down from the cushion and gave his shoulder a shove, and he rolled to his hands and knees. He was halfway standing before he even realized he was awake, grabbing at his belt like he was trying to draw a sword. "Droko, stop! You're dreaming."

He flinched visibly, then straightened and shook himself out.

"Are you okay?"

"I'm fine," he snapped. He was eyeing the wall as if he wasn't quite sure it could be trusted.

"Bad dream?" I asked cautiously. "You can tell me. Maybe it'll make you feel better."

He barked a humorless laugh. "I'd never give a dream any power over me by voicing its nonsense."

Wow, that was a far cry from Taruut, who loved regaling me with tales of his nocturnal wanderings—ramblings where he could still walk...and see. Guess they did things different in the Two Swords Clan.

"Nonsense or not, I can't help but wonder what orcs dream

about."

Droko strode over to the decaying tapestry and gazed into the threads. I didn't think he was about to answer, so it surprised me when he said, "The walls were on fire. But not. See? Nonsense."

"Well, it *is* awfully hot in here. Maybe you were just incorporating the steamy atmosphere into your dream."

"It wasn't that. It was more about...the way the walls looked. Glowing orange. Like they *were* the flame. And in the distance, thunder. But I knew the coming rain wasn't enough to stop me from burning alive."

Before I could say anything to put his mind at ease, someone pounded on the stone door. "Enter," Droko said gruffly.

Kof, the chief of the guard, came in and folded to his knees. "Droko the Sage, my spear is yours—"

Droko motioned impatiently for him to rise. "Yes, what is it?"

"The traveling peddler is here. Since you came here with only what you could carry—erm, that, and a goblin—I thought you'd want to know. He's waiting at the entry."

Curious to find out what an orcish merchant might sell, I followed Droko out. I paused only to scoop up my sullied shirt and slip it into the nearest brazier...only to wish I hadn't. The cave interior was hot, and thick with humidity, but out by the entrance, a wicked breeze cut through that raised goosebumps on my arms and hardened my nipples into fierce points.

The peddler's eyes went right to them.

And he wasn't an orc at all.

He was a few years older than me, though I couldn't place his exact age. His clothes had seen better days, but he wore his tattered lace with the unabashed pride of a lord in ermine. His reddish brown hair was too long to be practical, held back by a satin bow. But it was the way his eyes turned up at the corners that really piqued my interest.

While he might be no orc...I wasn't so sure he was a human, either. With his exotic good looks, no doubt he'd fetch a fine price at the red lantern and would never go to bed hungry.

Droko looked him up and down, nostrils flaring. I've never been able to afford the luxury of jealousy. But as I realized Droko was *smelling* this newcomer, my cheeks went hot with anger.

Oblivious—or maybe just used to it—the peddler sketched a deep bow with a ridiculously overdone flourish. "Pleased to make the acquaintance of this new shaman who's got everyone all abuzz. Name's Silver, costermonger extraordinaire. At your service, m'lord."

"I'm nobody's lord," Droko said gruffly. "It's Droko."

"Droko the Sage," snapped another orchish voice as Gargle emerged from a side tunnel. His nostrils flared, too.

But I wasn't entirely sure it was this Silver character he was sniffing.

Did he *know* what the shaman and I had been up to? I'd barely grazed him with the tip of my tongue....

Another breeze whistled through the cavern. Droko yanked off his doeskin cloak and threw it around my shoulders. I did my best not to preen in Gargle's smug face, truly I did. But that simple act of kindness touched me in a place I thought I'd walled off long ago.

To the peddler, Droko said, "Give the slave some proper clothing—at a fair price. Don't waste our time haggling."

A smile lit Silver's eyes. "I wouldn't dream of it."

There was a handcart behind him piled with the sorts of items all peddlers use to entice the attention of jaded buyers: colorful baubles, bits of carved shell and bone. But he'd also brought wares that an orc might find useful, like flasks, leatherwork, whetstones, and tools. Droko strode past him and pawed impatiently through his wares. He must not have found anything to his liking. With a grunt, he dropped a waterskin back into the cart, turned on his heel, and said to Gargle, "Don't disturb me unless the chieftain's here—or you've found the crypt."

I might not have the nose of an orc, but when I settled Droko's cloak more firmly around me, I could definitely smell something beyond just the fabric lining. Earthy, like turned soil and moss. Who ever thought orcs would smell so good?

Droko was an enigma, no two ways about it. When he was bossing folks around—his slaves, his guard, pretty much anyone but the chieftain—he barked out orders with the confidence of a flesh-peddler. But ask him an esoteric question, and he either froze up or shrugged it right off.

Fascinating.

"Well, then," Silver said briskly, dusting his hands together. "As I won't be permitted the indulgence of haggling, my visit will be brief. If there's anything you gentlemen should require...."

A few of the guardsmen poked through the wares, one replacing his tinderbox, another upgrading his belt buckle. And while Silver did keep an eye on them, he lavished the majority of his dubious attention on me.

"Does the slave have a name?" he asked teasingly.

He annoyed me already. "It's Archie."

"Ah. How fortunate for *Archie* that I cater to such a wide range of clientele...and that I'd heard there was a human here who might need a thing or two. Otherwise everything in today's selection would be orc-sized. Which would certainly present a challenge." His eyes twinkled in amusement. "As they're so very...*big*."

I quelled an eye-roll. I've been acquainted with plenty of guys like Silver. Always taunting, smirking, hinting that they know you better than you know yourself. Never mind that I'd so recently faced down the biggest dick I'd ever encountered—and I've encountered a *lot* of dick. There was no way he could actually know what I'd done last night.

At least, I hoped not. For both Droko's sake, and mine.

Silver rummaged through his handcart and came up with a shirt. It was a pale sea foam green that stood out amid the dull browns and grays of the handcart. The fabric was a fine weave, though it was somewhat thin around the elbows, and the buttons were tarnished. "This belonged to a pirate captain, who snuck it out of the royal palace in Esterhama before his ship was sunk by a rival fleet. It's been all around the world, even to distant islands that very few ever get to see." He paused and looked me up and down. "You know, I have the strangest feeling that this shirt is just the thing for you."

I crossed my arms. "It's huge. I'd drown in it."

"Ah." Silver's lips curved in a sly smile. "But that's what these lacings are for." He uncrossed my arms, divested me of my cloak, and tugged it over my head in a fluid motion as he swung around behind me. When he grabbed up the laces and cinched them tight, the shirt molded itself to me like a second skin.

"There." He stepped back to assess his handiwork. "Very

flattering, indeed." His grin broadened. "*Green* seems to suit you."

The eye-roll I'd been so successful at tamping down forced its way to the surface.

"Of course," the peddler added, "if you were hoping for something dull and utilitarian, I could scour the bottom of my wagon and see if there's a rag or two I can spare."

"I'm sure it'll do."

He indicated my arm with the jut of his pointy chin—the arm I'd scraped within an inch of its life shoving my way through cracks in the cave walls. "Just make sure you don't bleed on the fabric. Blood stains are notoriously stubborn to get out."

His tone was light...but now his eyes were searching mine in a way that wasn't entirely mocking. He thought someone here was being rough with me.

I liked his pity even less than his mockery.

"I'll be fine," I said firmly. "Besides, it's not as if anyone will pay attention to what a slave is wearing when they're all wrapped up in the funeral rites."

Silver arched an eyebrow. "Orcs kill each other so efficiently, I've never known them to trouble themselves with rites. Just throw the carcass on the fire and move on to the next battle."

"Not every orc is a fighter."

"Ah, so the old man hasn't set off on the rest of his journey yet. I was very fond of Taruut, you know. Once his eyesight faded, he developed quite the sweet tooth. I always made sure to save a bit of honeycomb just for him."

I suddenly missed Taruut terribly—how he'd laugh when I got an orcish custom totally wrong, and the way he would turn a mundane conversation into an impromptu lesson on some esoteric topic like herbal remedies or plant identification.

But at least now he was safe from harm. Unlike Droko, who'd be a lot bloodier than my arm if he couldn't find the shaman's crypt.

"The funeral is tomorrow." I hoped it would be, anyhow

"Well, then. Perhaps I will stay and pay my respects. After all, nothing says goodbye like one last hurrah."

Fantastic.

"In the meanwhile," he said, "your friend Quinn asked me to deliver this."

His leather vest was so covered in buckles and lacings, I didn't even see the pocket until he teased his long, tapered fingers into the opening and withdrew a note on a scrap of bark-paper. Was Quinn planning another escape—one he couldn't dare whisper about in earshot of the chieftain? I wasn't entirely sure how I felt about that. Probably because it would complicate matters to take him with me when I carved my way to freedom.

I was so sure Quinn had sent me some illicit plans that when I unfolded the slip of paper, I was baffled by what was actually there.

A recipe.

"What's this supposed to be?"

Silver made a big show of seeing the note for the first time—as if he didn't know damn well what was on it—and said, "It's called Easewater. Dreamweed, a very potent, very specific numbing agent. Night laurel—very relaxing. And rocknut oil, so delightfully slippery—and sure to last all... night...long."

If this guy thought talking about lube would make me blush, he could think again.

Silver fluttered his eyelashes. "If you haven't got all the ingredients, I may be able to dredge up—"

"I'm sure the shaman's apothecary stores can handle it."

"Very good. But just so you're aware...." He found a shard of graphite somewhere in his overcomplicated getup, grabbed the note from me, flipped it over, and began to write as he spoke. "There are two ways the potion might be mixed. Juice the night laurel and add the oil, and the two very different ingredients bind together in such a way as make a most unique—and delightful—blend." He sketched some kind of stirring motion. "But if it turns out things don't mix properly, you'll have a real mess on your hands. In that case, it's best to scrap the whole thing."

"I'll keep that in mind."

Silver handed me the paper. As he did, he held my gaze just a moment too long. So quietly I could barely hear it, he added, "I could never be a slave. No matter how finely gilded the cage."

I glanced down at his sketch and saw he hadn't been talking about mixing potions at all—but warning me to leave if things went wrong. And they weren't instructions he'd scribbled on the back after all...but a map. Once I oriented myself, I recognized the cave. The village wall. And beside that was a meandering path—one which presumably led to freedom.

I stuffed the note into my waistband. Since I'd spent the night with Droko, I'd been of two minds about leaving—but not anymore. Maybe it was the contrarian in me, but this offer to help me escape only made me more determined to stick around. "I don't need your plan. Call it a cage if you will. But I know full well what's beyond these walls." Pointedly, I swung Droko's cloak around my shoulders. "At least here, someone actually cares about me."

"Never mind, then." Silver tilted his head and smiled a cryptic smile. "I thought the shaman's grand gesture of giving you his cloak was just a clever way to put his scent on you—and cover his own tracks. My mistake...I'm sure you know best."

15

DROKO

My time was growing short. While everyone was busy with the merchant, I sought out Crespash in Taruut's chambers to see what he'd found.

"A whole lot of nothing."

The slave lounged on the old shaman's sedan chair, experimentally gumming a dried mushroom. There was an empty wineskin beside him. I quelled the urge to dump him off the chair myself. A passing guard might notice, and wonder why I hadn't ordered *him* to beat the goblin for me, instead.

"Then what are you doing here? Shouldn't you be out looking?"

"I did look. Just like I was told. Found plenty of mushrooms, but no crypt."

He pushed a few onto the floor as he rose, and I had to grit my teeth not to roar at him. "Do you think this is some kind of joke?"

"Goblin senses are notoriously acute...all but the sense of humor. In fact, I find the situation very serious indeed. Just came round to check your captain's map and make sure I didn't spend my day treading in someone else's footsteps. I presume you're hard at work on your own search." He leered at me...and I wondered if what I'd done with Archie was so easy to see. "Pray tell, Droko the Sage, what have *you* discovered?"

"That I've got no time to waste squabbling with you. Now, track down that crypt or we're both as good as dead."

The goblin would have stuck around to get in a few more licks—he's notoriously disobedient—but when he put a stubby hand to the ground to read the caves' vibrations, he quickly changed his mind and set off. Just as he eeled out of a narrow passage, the sound of metal-clad boots on stone reached my ears. Since my own guard wore sandals, it could only be the chieftain's men.

And Ul-Rott was with them.

The shaman's chambers were hung all around with bundles of drying herbs, and the chieftain swatted away a fern frond tickling at his cheek. He was a warrior, accustomed to grand halls and wide open spaces. The steamy, dark closeness of the caves didn't sit well on his armored shoulders. So it was curious he should visit twice in as many days.

"I still have until dawn to find that crypt," I blurted out, and his guard's eyes widened at my directness. "Er...Praise Ul-Rott," I added, wondering if I'd just exposed myself as a chieftain's son...albeit a disposable third one.

"Yes, of course. I may not be known for my patience, but I do know how to count. I'm following up on yesterday's visit. I need more of that salve."

"I'm pleased to hear it worked." Hopefully he didn't expect me to whip up another batch on the spot. "It's a tedious process to create, but the proof is in the results. I'll send some to your lodge as soon as it's ready."

The chieftain grunted his agreement, eyeing a shelf of dried animal paws with a puzzled scowl on his face. I was relieved he wasn't hoping to view my poor attempt at herbcraft...until I realized he could just have easily sent word with a guard instead of walking over here himself. Especially given the state of his inner thighs.

"Not only a tedious process," I said, "but lengthy."

Ul-Rott turned to me in assessment. "Men say shamans have one foot in the spirit world—do they make these claims in Two Swords?"

"Some do."

"You're blunt. An uncommon trait for a shaman."

Unease twisted my gut.

"Not just blunt," he went on, "but plainspoken. Back before your former clan tried to claim our lands—back when it was safe for orcs to mingle with our distant brethren—I'd get envoys from other clans as far off as the Wasteland. I even visited a few myself. And all their shamans had the same gift: turning plain speech into a tangle of nonsense. They could hardly tell someone water was wet without making a whole production out of it."

Crespash had warned me about my plain speech. But I had no talent for embellishment. As much as I needed my goblin to find that crypt, right now I wished I had him whispering in my ear. "I've never seen the point in wasting breath on useless words."

"Not very politic of you, I'll say that much. It will take some getting used to. Not that I'd ever mix you up with Taruut. The old man was practically a skeleton. Had to be carted around everywhere on his chair. But you...." He eyed me up and down. "So big I might mistake you for one of your honor guard, if it weren't for your trinkets and your staff."

I was suddenly very aware of the tree branch propped against the wall, and the ridiculous bits of feather and grass the goblin had shoved into my outfit on our hasty trek through the woods.

The chieftain's eyes went shrewd, and I regretted giving away my cloak. "You stand more like a soldier than a priest."

I knew better than to contradict the chieftain, so responded as I would with my father, with a single nod.

"Well," Ul-Rott said brusquely. "I'm more comfortable around soldiers, anyway. Who's got time to sift through a bunch of cryptic remarks searching for the truth?"

"Agreed." I might actually come through this meeting unscathed. I steered the chieftain around a work table, toward the exit. "So I will send over your remedy when it's done. But now I must prepare for the funeral rites—"

"Hold on, shaman. I didn't come all this way just to pat you on the back."

He looked at me expectantly.

I hadn't the faintest notion what to make of it. "You say you value bluntness," I said. "As do I. What is it you want?"

He gestured to the spot at my hip where my sword hilt used to hang—which now bore an entirely different weight. "Whenever I saw Taruut alone, he'd end the visit by tossing the ivories."

A dozen excuses sprang to mind, but none of them felt plausible. It would be an insult to remind him that I was *not* Taruut after he'd just spent so long remarking about that very thing. This was Ul-Rott's clan. And it was clear I was expected to do things his way.

And so I swallowed hard, plucked the bag from my belt, and dumped its contents on the table.

As the teeth scattered, I held my breath. My pulse pounded in my ears. Through that, the sound of teeth clacking against stone dragged my fitful dream to the surface again. The walls were fire. In the distance, thunder. Followed by rain.

"Even your milk teeth are big," the chieftain remarked.

But I hardly heard him over the clatter echoing through my mind. "The sky will mourn Taruut's passing," I found myself saying to prevent him from asking about the crypt.

Ul-Rott cocked his head as if trying to deduce whatever pattern I'd seen in the teeth. Or maybe he'd spied the pebble among them. "Are you sure?" he said. I quickly scooped the "ivories" into the pouch. The chieftain hadn't seemed to notice the stone. "There's not a cloud in the sky."

Why hadn't I predicted something more ambiguous? I could hardly back down now. It would only make me look weak. So, I dredged up a phrase my father's shaman always used. "In the dark, your feet must find the path with no help from your eyes." As far as I was concerned it was an awfully precious way of saying, *Who knows?* But it did sound the part.

"I'll never ken to the ways of a shaman," Ul-Rott chortled with a shake of his head. "Unnatural, if you ask me. But knowing the weather before it happens would give me a fine advantage on the battlefield. So we'll see if this brash prediction of yours comes to pass."

The chieftain turned to go, and I released that breath I'd been holding. But before my heart could stop trying to pound through my ribcage, Ul-Rott paused in the doorway and added, "And you'd better pray to your ancestors it rains."

16

ARCHIE

No one challenged me as I hurried toward the kitchen. Why would they? I'd been preparing the shaman's meals since he arrived, and frankly, I'm sure the big, strapping orcs had better things to do than worry about one puny human slave.

The last meal I'd prepared, I sifted through all the ingredients looking for something to impress Droko. This time, though, the only thing I cared about was portability.

I needed food—all I could carry. Because once I carved just a few more steps...I was *so* outta there.

Stupid cloak.

While the shaman's pantry held nothing overtly useful like hardtack or jerky, there were some supplies that would travel well: dried fruits and nuts, coarse bread, and even some leathery mushrooms. I gathered as much as I thought I could carry without being noticed. Hopefully, if any of my captors smelled the food on me, they would just think I picked up the scent in the kitchen.

The green shirt I bought from Silver, even with its laces and ties, had absolutely nowhere to hide a bundle of provisions. *Droko's* cloak would do the job—but I'd left it hanging by the kitchen door with no intention of putting it back on.

Why would I have simply tossed such a valuable garment aside? It was cold out there in the big, bad world outside the steamy confines of these caves. And if I'd gone off without it, surely I'd be sorry by the time the sun set. What compelled me to even dream of abandoning the silly garment anyhow?

Obviously, I wasn't *angry* about the damn thing. It's not like I actually *cared* that the gift was only a way to cover his scent. I never *expected* him to think of me as something more than a passing diversion. I wasn't some starry-eyed virgin who'd fall in *love* with the first man he bedded. In fact, I should be thanking Droko—cloaking myself with his scent might very well make me harder to track.

Really, if anything, he'd done me a massive favor.

"Thanks a lot," I said under my breath as I stomped back to the kitchen and grabbed the damn cloak from its peg. I did my best to ignore the earthy scent of rain on moss that billowed out from the lining when I snapped it open.

As I latched the bundle to the back of my belt and covered it with Droko's cloak, a scrap of paper fluttered to the floor. The peddler's hasty map. Except, when I picked it up, the map side wasn't facing me. The potion was. Dreamweed. Night Laurel. Rocknut oil. The first two ingredients would be in Taruut's apothecary, not the kitchen. But I might find the rocknut oil....

No—I wasn't about to start looking. There was no reason to look. None. I took a decisive step back from the shelves. It didn't matter whether I'd seen that damn oil here or not.

I was leaving. And that was that.

The corridors and the caves were familiar now. I kept my lantern low and my ears pricked for the sound of footsteps. Size might be an advantage for orcs when it came to combat, but it made them a lot easier to hear.

I felt my way along the dim tunnel by memory and instinct, and found the passageway leading to the crescent-shaped gap much sooner than I'd hoped. My heart pounded with the anticipation of finally being free, and my stomach filled with butterflies. Not over the regret of leaving Droko, obviously. I'm sure it was just nerves.

I rounded the final corner, eager to squeeze my way to the petrified men and carve out those last few steps, only to be startled by a pair of huge, glowing eyes shining through the darkness. I let out an undignified yelp and scrambled backward, opening my lantern wide to flood the passage with light. The creature standing between me and the crescent-shaped gap merely winced as protective membranes slipped over his bulging eyeballs.

"Crespash," I said disdainfully. "What are you doing here?"

"I could ask you the same thing, human."

"I'm looking for the crypt, just like everyone else."

"And exactly how far had you planned to explore? Far enough to require a meal?" His oversized eyes flicked to the bulge beneath the cloak. "*Several* meals?"

"That's none of your concern."

"I'd be remiss to fail to notice you're drowning in sweat from that heavy cloak. Such delicate things, humans. Always hungry or tired, hot or cold—how you survive with such fussy constitutions, I'll never know. Dwarves, on the other hand...." He fanned the stumps of his fingers for emphasis. "Now, there's a sturdy people."

I'd known a dwarf, back in Wildwood. Saucy little thing, and her company fetched a fine price. But the scenarios her customers dreamed up for her were disturbing, to say the least.

"What?" the goblin prompted. "You don't believe in dwarves?"

"Of course I do."

"I'm not talking about the occasional human runt, but the folk those stunted humans are named for. True dwarves. The ones who wrote this." He plucked something out of his leathers and held it up for my inspection: a tightly rolled scroll.

"I gave that to Droko."

"And he tossed it aside. To him, no doubt, it looked like a bunch of random ticks and dings. Dwarves have their own way of setting down words."

"Which you just so happen to know how to read."

"Of course I do. Dwarven Burrowers are highly sought after by those of us who live underground. They can carve a rock thin enough to see the glow of a candle through it. They know exactly where to dig to keep the ceiling from coming down on their heads. And they can blend a trap into a cave wall so cunning that even a goblin wouldn't see it till their innards were pooling around their feet.

"Dwarvish contracts are notoriously thorough. It behooves a goblin to know what they're getting into if they sign one.

"Though not all dwarvish writing is purely practical. They're especially fond of penning their own histories, for instance—though those tales are infamously long-winded and dull. But once in a while, if you're lucky, you'll run across some very bawdy dwarvish poetry."

"Is that what you're wasting my time over?" I asked, with way more bravado than I actually felt. "Poetry?"

"Sadly, no. But since the dwarf didn't have enough room to go into excruciating detail here, we're left with a telling that made for a surprisingly good read." When I shifted uneasily, the membranes on his eyes peeled open and he looked me up and down. "What's wrong, human...got somewhere to be?"

"We should be looking for the crypt. Not dallying over some random curiosity."

"Ah, but here's the thing. This wee bit of random curiosity might be more valuable than you think."

Obviously, now I had to know. "Fine. What does it say?"

The goblin unrolled the tight cylinder of parchment with his finger-stumps, and read.

Two moons have passed since our labor was finished—and two of my comrades have passed as well. As our reward for crafting the tomb of their heathen shamans, our orcish captors have sealed us up to die in the very caves we helped them shape.

We were fools to think a slave of the orcs could ever earn his freedom. The shaman promised us our lives, and orcs have a reputation for being true to their word. But then, the shaman was laid to rest. Along with him, so went the promises he'd made.

If we had our equipment, we could drill our way out. But once the tomb was complete, their blacksmith melted our picks and hammers to slag. We have no tools, no food, and no water, save for the trickle of condensation we can capture from the walls.

The only thing of value the orcs didn't take from us was Dreadforge.

Crespash glanced up from the scroll. "Dwarves name their sacred weapons, you see. When the blades are pulled from the smithy's flames, they're quenched in the guts of a living enemy to imbue the metal with the poor sod's very soul. If you believe in that kind of thing...which, apparently, the orcs did, if they didn't confiscate the sword along with all their other tools."

Dreadforge. I'd spent hours with the heavy sword carving my way to freedom. It was like learning one of your favorite paying men was caught with a dead whore in his bed...and realizing that could've easily been you. Creepy. But if the dwarves considered the blade sacred, that did explain why they didn't use it to cut their own path out.

Crespash was watching for my reaction, but I gave him my blankest stare. He turned back to the scroll and read some more.

I've thought long and hard about using Dreadforge to ease my last companion's suffering, but it would be a dishonor, and I cannot give in to the temptation. Instead, we worked together to build our own biers, prying loose the stone with our daggers. The final bier, mine, is nearly complete. When the time comes, I will lay myself to rest with Dreadforge in my hand, and prepare to be judged by the Great Smith, and hopefully deemed worthy to throw myself upon his forge.

How will the gods of our captors judge them? I've heard they have no gods, and pray only to their ancestors. That would explain why they care nothing for honor. The wretched orcs can deprive us of our tools, our freedom, and even our lives. But my honor is something they can never take away.

Crespash flapped the bit of parchment. "A lot to digest from such a tiny slip of hide. You see the density of the dings and dots of their writing. Now imagine a whole book of the stuff. It'll knock you out faster than a sleeping draught. But the question is...where did you find the scroll?"

"On the floor." The lie came easily. It was the standard reply by the red lantern, where besotted customers might lavish you with their family heirlooms while they were in their cups, then accuse you of having stolen them once the drink wore off.

"I suppose you never know what sorts of valuable items might simply be scattered around for the taking. Take, for instance...an impressive lump of stormsilver."

"What's that, some other dwarvish thing I've never heard of?"

"Not as such, though they'd pay a pretty penny for the chance at working the stuff into one of their weapons. It so happens that Droko has a piece of it almost as big as that lunch you're doing such a bad job of hiding."

"Forget about the food. Do you realize what this scroll means? There's definitely a crypt here somewhere. It's just very well hidden."

"And if you're the one to help Droko the Sage find it, no doubt he'll shower you with adulation and cherish you forever. Is that what you're thinking?" He didn't have to be such a dick about it. "Well, think again. He's an orc. You're not. He'll never think of you as anything more than a slave."

And yet, when Quinn fingered that heavy gold chain and spoke of Marok....

"Now, before you warm to the idea that being Droko's slave might actually have its perks—yes, I'd need to be blind not to see you mooning over each other—you'll want to hear the rest of the scroll."

"There's more?"

"There is, indeed." Crespash fixed me with a meaning-ful look, then eased open just the bottom and read, *An undignified ending. I should have expected no less from a barbaric race that buries its slaves alive with its masters.*"

As he spoke each fateful word, Crespash took a step forward, and I took one step back. By the time he'd finished the ugly pronouncement, my ass was up against the unyielding surface of the tunnel wall and the goblin was way too close for comfort. I couldn't read him. I'm great at reading men—even orcs. But I was at a loss. Was this a show of dominance? A threat? Or—stars help me—was that gummy, gray mouth closing in to seal our deal with a kiss?

I flinched, hard—horrified by the *kissing* thought most of all—just as the goblin struck. He was about my height, but that's where the similarity ended. His arms were long and gangly, and he moved faster than any human I'd ever seen. Lucky for me, he had terrible aim.

Or, did he?

He stepped back, clutching something to his chest that he'd plucked from the wall beside my head. It squirmed and writhed, trying to wrest itself from the goblin's grasp, but despite his lack of proper fingers, he managed to hold on tight. I had no idea what it might be until a spindly leg popped free, and then I recognized it for what it was: a spider. Not the common creatures that nested in the cracks of the walls at the brothel, but a monstrous thing like the husks I'd encountered in the old pantry.

Those dried shells had been creepy, but to see it all fleshed out and moving was downright horrifying. You'd think all those legs would be the worst part—or even the fangs. But it was the flesh that made my skin crawl. Unlike the whitish remains of the dead spiders, the shell of the living creature was see-through. And the guts underneath were translucent and pink, like the meat of a boiled prawn, with a sickening webwork of colored veins pulsing through it.

Without thinking, I went for the dwarven dagger I'd been hiding, and managed to clear it from my breeches without cutting an artery. But instead of being glad for my help, Crespash *hissed* at me and said, "Don't you dare!"

"But—"

He caught one of the flailing legs, trapping them all to the body, then brought the writhing creature to his lips and blew a puff of air between its clicking mandibles. The bug stiffened. Not entirely still—it was twitching vaguely—but most definitely subdued.

"The Opal Widow is a rarity in these parts. The peddler could get a good price for it—and no doubt he's got a thing or two we'll need if we plan to survive out there."

"If you say so." I shuddered.

Crespash dropped his gaze to the dagger in my hand. "I suppose you found that on the floor, too," he said with a smirk. "You're resourceful, I'll give you that. Tell you what—procure the stormsilver for me and I'll make sure we both make it out of this wretched pit alive."

I reluctantly agreed. With him standing between me and my hidden sword—Dreadforge—I didn't have much choice. Bad enough he knew I'd "found" the scroll. I shifted my grip on the dagger to hide the workmanship, in case the hilt was obviously dwarvish.

"I used to have ten such lovely weapons," Crespash said, "right on the ends of my very own fingers. That's what happens when you get caught stealing from orcs."

"In Wildwood they'd take your whole hand."

"Ah, but the orcs weren't using me as an example. They

were just trying to make sure I was defenseless so I couldn't tear out their throats as they slept." He nodded toward the dagger. "You keep that little claw, human. I've nowhere to put it. And besides...." He flashed his gray gums at me. "I think you're gonna need it."

17

DROKO

The sun was lowering on the horizon when I saw Ul-Rott out of the caves. My sense of time was off-kilter from spending so long underground. One look at the purpling sky—just as cloudless as the chieftain had claimed—filled me with urgency and dread. If I didn't find the crypt by morning, the old shaman would have to go on a funeral pyre, like a lowly soldier.

And Ul-Rott would stoke the flames with my headless corpse.

I strode back to the chalk map, searching desperately for some way we'd overlooked. No doubt the answer was right there. I just needed to see it.

I was on my hands and knees, following a sinuous path with my fingertip, when the sound of orcish footfalls paused in the entryway. I glanced up and found Kof regarding me with some confusion through his single eye. "Droko the Sage," he said quickly, touching the ground with his bent knee. "Are you well?"

"I'm fine." Though I wouldn't be for much longer if we

didn't find that crypt.

"Please." He sidestepped a chalk line and then hovered at my side, as if searching for some way to help me up without actually touching my sacred person. "This is the work of servants. It's not fit for a shaman."

I pushed back into a ready crouch, planting my elbows on my knees. "Time is running out. Unless you have something useful to add."

Kof squatted beside me. "I have been scouting the northernmost tunnel...." He hesitated.

"And?"

He pointed at another of the markings with a wince. "And it loops around, and exits here."

The last two potential routes...both of them useless.

"Then that's it. We've explored every possible passage big enough for an orc, and not one of them leads to a crypt. There must be something we've overlooked." I turned back to the map, hoping to find any gap that might contain a crypt.

Kof shifted uneasily.

I glanced up, finding his scarred brow furrowed with concern. "What is it?"

"It's not my place to say."

"You're the captain of my guard. If you don't tell me what you think, then who will?"

He pondered his words for a moment, then forced himself to speak. "Any of us can stare at this map. Even me...with a single eye. But the only one able to hear the whispers of the ancestors is you."

Meditation. A shaman's solution to any problem. But the last thing I wanted to do was sit on my thumb and pretend to be receiving some esoteric wisdom. I was no man of thought, only action. If I wanted the orcs to believe I was a shaman, though, I'd need to play along. At least until Kof ventured back into the caves so that I could resume my strategizing in peace.

When I made my way to the meditation chamber, my mind was on the tunnels as I dragged my fingertips across the cool stone wall. I couldn't see much of anything by the tricky light of a lantern. Surely, it was possible the guardsmen missed something. Unless they touched every surface, a narrow passage, a hidden gap, would be easy enough to overlook. If only I could go back to the map and take another—

A figure stood in the open door of my sanctuary, backlit by a flickering brazier. Taruut come to visit from beyond the veil of death? A ridiculous notion that I immediately dismissed. All this talk of visions and ancestors had clearly gone to my head. I raised my lantern and threw open the shutter....

Only to see it was Gorgul waiting for me in the chamber.

Of all the guards, he was the most ambitious. If anyone had made progress, it would be him. "Did you find anything?" I asked.

A pleased smile wrapped itself around his tusks. "I'd say so."

It looked like I would manage to live another day, after all....

At least until Gorgul tossed me something distinctly head-shaped, and I realized it was the source of my "ivories."

Dropping the skull, I stiffened and drew myself up to my full height—Ul-rott was right, I did make a better soldier than a shaman. But as such, I could see that without armor, without a weapon, I stood no chance at all against the spear in Gorgul's hand. The honor guard was supposed to *be* my weapon.

I would have preferred a sword. Unless you're phenomenally clumsy, cold steel won't bite you in the back.

"Don't worry, *Droko the Sage*," Gorgul sneered. "I'd be an idiot to do you any harm. Especially when there's so much *you* can do for me."

He invited me into my own sanctuary with exaggerated politeness, then rolled the stone over the doorway to seal us both in.

I squared my shoulders and declared, "I am your shaman. You are the one in service. Not I."

Gorgul's stance didn't change in the slightest. He was relaxed and confident. Even bored.

"Here's how it's gonna work," he said. "First of all, we pick out some dusty, out-of-the-way corner no one's bothered with for ages. We throw some old bones inside, then smoke up the place with so much incense, Ul-rott won't be able to see the tips of his own tusks, let alone what's in the room. You chant your nonsense and shake your stick and make a good show of putting the old man to rest. And once it's all said and done, you get rid of that one-eyed fool and appoint me as your new captain."

It was a sensible plan...which made it all the worse. I'd approached the situation like an obedient soldier, and I'd just presumed Taruut's honor guard would be the same. All the while, Gorgul had been scheming to get ahead.

All these years of being drilled in duty and respect.... I had a lot to unlearn.

"Don't look so disappointed," Gorgul said. "Won't it feel good to stop pretending? Do as I say, and I'll leave you be.

You can carry on spewing your fake predictions and dicking your slaves. And everyone will be happy."

Did he know about Archie, or was he just probing for weaknesses? He was only half-right—I'd just as soon fornicate with a wild boar as touch the goblin—but I steeled my expression so as not to give anything away. Too bad I couldn't quell the desperate pounding of my own heart. And as Gorgul glanced into the brazier where scraps of Archie's shirt remained, I suspected it was no guess.

I flexed my fingers, eager to grab him by the throat and jam his smug face into the stony wall—to tell him that if any harm came to Archie, his skull would be the next one rolling across the sanctuary floor. But he was armed and I was not. And even if I did somehow slay him, I'd have trouble explaining the death of my guardsman within my own walls.

"There's still time to find the real crypt," I said coldly. "Now, go."

Gorgul complied—but with a smirk that told me he only left because he wanted to.

The situation was hopeless. The more I sought to defend Archie, the more likely he'd be used as leverage against me. I itched to do something, anything, to help myself. But I was stuck playing the shaman, and could only pace around the ridiculous cushion where I was expected to meditate. I'd practically worn a path into the floor when the heavy stone door clicked and began to roll aside.

I expected it was Gorgul, come to give me his next command. But the scent of human reached my nose half a heartbeat before I realized the man joining me was Archie.

Relief swept through me at the sight of him—whole, and more than that, well. He'd shed his cadet linens for human garb. It was only clothing. And yet, now he looked not just older and more mature—but far more exotic.

Even beautiful.

"Is it time for breakfast already?" I asked.

"Not quite. I just wanted to see how you're doing." How human of him. And strangely heartwarming—which made no sense. My attachment to him only made me more vulnerable...and yet, his presence kindled such hope in my heart.

Grown orcs didn't tend to each other's *feelings*. I would never think to ask the chieftain if he felt trepidation over an upcoming battle—even if he was my own father. Or to see if my captain wanted moral support over an unexpected defeat. The only person I would even imagine speaking with about such things was my bride...the one stolen from me by my brother.

Which somehow mattered much less to me whenever I was with this fragile human.

Archie eased up to me. His gait was distractingly graceful, and his eyes raked my body. His tone was a light banter. "If you're hungry, I could go put something together...."

Who could think about food right now, anyway? "Never mind about that." I tore my gaze from the delicate hollow of his throat. "Actually, I want to know your thoughts about something."

"The wise, all-knowing shaman seeks the council of a lowly human food taster? This ought to be good."

"You've been here longer than I have." More importantly, I trusted his motives. "Can we dress up an unused chamber and pass it off as a crypt? Or will Ul-Rott have our heads?"

Archie's brow furrowed—human faces were so expressive. "It's a huge gamble. The chieftain didn't get where he is by being stupid."

"But he is as eager as anyone to lay Taruut to rest. He may believe what he wants to believe."

"That's an awfully risky presumption."

"I've walked these passageways myself. There's plenty of old—" I almost said *junk*. "Old artifacts we could gather into the semblance of a tomb. There are bones everywhere. The walls are covered in them. Arrange them cunningly enough, wrap some bundles of twigs in a shroud, and there you have it—a succession of dead shamans. Surround them with necessities they would need for their journey across the veil—"

"Y'know what?" Archie blurted out. "I think you're onto something."

It seemed an awfully abrupt change of heart, given how skeptical he'd been just a moment before.

But Archie quickly warmed to the idea. "There *are* quite a few spots where no one has ventured for a very long time. Quite possibly longer than Ul-Rott has been chieftain. Since Taruut was older than dirt, I doubt many orcs around here have been to the last shaman's funeral. And if they question your methods, you can just claim things were done differently in the Two Swords Clan. It's perfect."

He dusted his hands together as if he was eager to get to work and lavished me with a broad, encouraging smile.

It might have put my mind at ease...had his scent not soured with anxiety when he added, "Especially if you dress it up with your stormsilver."

His eyes raked my body yet again. Not to fantasize about what the two of us had done, I realized. But to figure out where I carried the lump of metal. "You've been talking with Crespash."

"He may have mentioned it within my earshot, yes."

So, the two of them were working together. And the most obvious reason slaves would be in collusion would be to plan an escape.

How ridiculous of me to think the human was actually concerned about me.

The only thing on his mind was finding a way out.

"You do have it," Archie said, all innocence. "Don't you?"

Brusquely, I said, "It's no business of yours. Now, leave me. I have a funeral to deal with."

I wasn't exactly surprised that Archie was planning an escape...more like profoundly disappointed. If we somehow made it through the interment ritual and I went along with Gorgul's schemes, I told myself, I would end up right where I'd wanted. The Two Swords Clan would be safe. And I would not only have my own household here, but my own dominion.

Too bad the mere thought of it left me feeling hollowed out and empty.

The day caught up to me—or maybe the night. Who could tell what time it was anymore, lurking around in steamy, sunless tunnels that reeked of sulfur. It might even be time for breakfast—the meal that Archie never made—and soon the chieftain would show up with Taruut's body...and my fate would be sealed. Either Ul-Rott would see through my ruse and relieve me of my head—or I'd succeed, only to live out my days as Gorgul's puppet.

It was tempting to pull out the stormsilver and see if it held any answers for me in its crackling depths, but the tingle that raced up my arm when I slipped a finger into my belt pouch changed my mind. I squatted gingerly, closing my eyes, hoping some other path would present itself. But try as I might, I could think of no other way.

I must have nodded off, for as I searched, I dreamed.

And all the walls pulsed with flame.

18

ARCHIE

Did I think Droko's plan for faking a tomb would work? Maybe. Too bad I couldn't stick around long enough to find out. Real or fake, a tomb is a tomb. I had no intention of being sealed in and ending up like those petrified dwarves. Especially when Droko had just proved exactly how much I meant to him by refusing me the stormsilver.

No matter. While Crespash was busy unloading the spider, I'd take a few more swings with Dreadforge and cut my way to freedom.

If I could ever manage to reach the sword, anyhow.

Avoiding the orcish guards was bad enough at the best of times. But now they were tromping all over the place with armloads of pottery and bones. The sound of their footsteps echoed so it sounded like they were coming from nowhere and everywhere. And if ever I needed to escape their notice, it was now.

So, naturally, I turned a corner thinking I was in the clear, and nearly collided with a seven-foot-tall lump of orc flesh. Lucky for me, not only was the huge mound of artifacts he carried blocking his sight—but he only had one eye.

Kof.

The captain didn't delight in tormenting me—not like Gargle—but I still couldn't risk him catching me so far from the kitchen.

The natural caves in this section were rough and the flickering lantern light danced over the surface, throwing tricky shadows as I flattened myself to the wall without a sound. It probably wouldn't do much good—the orc would be able to smell me—but I wasn't about to stand there and volunteer to be searched.

Unfortunately, judging by the echoes, Kof wasn't the only orc I'd need to avoid.

I pulled the shaman's cloak around me more tightly with one hand and scrabbled at the wall behind me with the other. With raw fingertips, I probed the rough stone, hoping some hidden dwarvish doorway would come to my rescue. No such luck, but I did find a shallow crevice where I could tuck myself away, hold my breath, and pray to all the gods I didn't believe in that I'd somehow manage to be overlooked.

Two more guards rounded a corner. Kof halted them, lowered his voice, and said, "This plan of the shaman's...it's a big risk. If the chieftain finds out—"

"Who would tell him?" Dang, I knew that voice: Gargle. I pressed myself into that crack so hard I practically sodomized myself on a stalagmite. "If the new shaman fails, we all fail. And none of us want to bear the chieftain's wrath."

"But there's still time to find the real crypt," Kof insisted. "I will speak to the shaman—"

"He'll see no one. He was very clear."

"Maybe so. But he's new to this clan—and so young. If I

don't offer my council—"

"And shame him by mistrusting his decisions?" Gargle said with a scoff. "Nothing leads to failure faster than disrespecting the shaman."

Kof grunted thoughtfully. "Good thing I have a second in command who sees things from every angle. It's not the first time you've saved me from myself, and I'm sure it won't be the last."

I risked a glance to see if I was alone, only to find Gargle and one of the other guards had paused to shift their grip on a huge jug of oil. I quickly ducked back into my crevice. Once Kof's footfalls receded, Gargle said to his parting steps, "No...I'm definitely done making you look good."

"What's that supposed to mean?" the other orc wondered.

"The shaman is getting rid of Kof. I made sure of it."

"Oh?" Gargle's crony sounded amused. "And how did you manage that?"

My nemesis pitched his voice low and nasty, and said, "What's the worst thing I could hold over the pup's head— something that would get him marched straight to the chopping block?"

Hold on. Gorgul *wasn't* on Droko's side?

"Is the new shaman a traitor?" the other guardsman guessed. "Ooh, I'll bet he is."

"What do you mean?"

"He's using his dark magic to sabotage Ul-Rott. Why, I'll wager those festering crotch-boils everyone's whispering about were the lad's way of getting revenge for stealing him away from his own clan—"

"Don't be stupid. That's impossible."

The crony warmed to his own idea. "Never smart to get

on the bad side of a shaman. You remember the poor sod who insulted Taruut, ended up trampled by an elk? Took a hoof straight through the kidney and died by morning. If that's not bad enough, they say his corpse was pissing blood."

"No one has magical dick boils," Gorgul said, "and no one's getting trampled. Even if Droko wanted to curse someone... he can't. The pup's not even a shaman."

No. No way. Gorgul was full of shit. He had to be. Because *of course* Droko was a shaman. Why else would he be here?

Droko...who never once gave me some cryptic shamanic answer...who didn't seem to know a mossberry from a mouse turd...who never so much as shook a bone in my direction.

Unless you counted the one between his legs.

And his assertion that he'd never taken an oath of celibacy.

A claim that suddenly made a lot more sense....

"Hold on." Gorgul made that distinctive whuffing noise an orc does when he's bathing his palate in scent. "I thought I smelled the shaman."

Belatedly, I realized I'd been clutching Droko's cloak around me so tightly my knuckles were white. I held my breath, worried they'd manage to scent my exhalation, and struggled against the cold sweat already prickling between my shoulder blades.

And then the other one whuffed. "Can't smell nothing but this reeking oil. Far as I'm concerned, we can't put this whole funeral business behind us soon enough. And if what you say is true—well, you'd better remember who your friends are when you're looking for your next lieutenant!"

I held my breath until my lungs clutched at my rib-cage and an image of the starry night sky painted itself against my closed eyelids. Lightheadedness tickled at my consciousness—I'd only recently recovered from my own malady, after all—but as I felt my knees threaten to buckle, the orcs hefted their burden and trudged off to the fake tomb.

I eased my way out of my hiding place and saw I was only a short jog away from the crescent-shaped gap. So close to freedom I could taste it. And yet...I couldn't just leave Droko to the jackals.

Hugging his cloak around me, I threw self-interest to the wind, kept my ears pricked for orcish footsteps, clung to the shadows...and made my way back to Droko.

He was still exactly where I'd left him, squatting in the meditation chamber, staring resolutely at the wall. "Forget breakfast—I'm not hungry."

Only after he got the words out did his nose register that breakfast had already been forgotten.

He turned to me and his nostrils flared. I didn't need to tell him I was totally unnerved, he could *smell* it. "What's wrong?" he asked cautiously as he got to his feet.

I understand men. The surest way to wound them isn't to kick them in the nuts, but to take a stab at their ego. But there was simply no time to do some delicate song and dance to coax a confession out of Droko, and pretend shock over learning he'd been living a lie. "I know," I said simply. "I know everything."

His expression went even grimmer than usual. "Then I suppose you have demands as well."

The accusation hit me like a slap. And still worse—I deserved it. Because I'd spent my whole life looking out only for myself. It was my nature—survival. But if taking off and leaving this man alone to fend off these vipers didn't qualify as betrayal, then I must've skipped that lesson somewhere along the way.

At least Droko didn't know I'd been planning to take his stormsilver and leave. If he ever found out, I'd surely die of shame. And I've always prided myself in being utterly shameless.

With confidence I didn't entirely feel, I said, "My only demand is that you get rid of Gorgul. Fire him, banish him. Whatever it takes."

Droko gave a heavy sigh. "He would talk."

"Then run him through with his own damn spear—"

"Archie," he said quietly...and the sound of my name in his deep orcish voice made me sway on my feet. "I don't claim to know how it is in human towns. But here, in the Red Hand Clan, if I slew him—there'd be consequences."

"But you can get away with anything! You're the shaman." At least as far as anyone knew.

"I'm a newcomer; Gorgul has been a respected member of this clan his whole life. Ul-Rott would have to investigate. All my secrets would be laid bare."

"You cured the chieftain's crotch! Surely, he'll look the other way."

Droko shook his head sadly. "To excuse the murder of a clan mate would undermine his authority. He'd have to make an example of me."

Was it too late to flee the caves with the rare dwarvish blade, whose sale would set me up for life with the best of everything money could buy? Maybe not. The only problem was, no matter how fine the house, the bed, the wine—how could I possibly enjoy any of it without Droko?

If I said what I was about to say, there'd be no going back...

but it had to be done. Before I could second-guess myself, I blurted out, "Come away with me, Droko."

He looked up sharply, confused. Impulsively, I dashed up to him and grabbed him by the hand. Obviously, I expected it to be bigger than mine. But it wasn't until I was actually clutching it that I appreciated how massive he was. A pair of his fingers were as big as my wrist, and his skin felt like hardened leather—but I didn't care that we were nothing alike. Because this was Droko. *My* Droko. Somehow, somewhere, we had to be able to carve out a life together.

And then, before I knew it, I was grappling him around the neck—by the stars, it was like climbing a tree!—and hauling myself up against him to press my mouth to his. Surprise was the only reason he moved at all, bowing his head so our lips could meet. All of the other orcs had tusks that could easily put out an eye, but not Droko. His curved ever so slightly outward. And when I went in for the kiss, they cupped my face like a lover's hand.

Droko's lips parted. Not in passion, but in wonder. In my long and sordid history, I'd certainly kissed men who didn't kiss me back. But now, that wasn't the case. Droko didn't exactly kiss me…but the thread of exhalation that played across my lower lip as his breath caught was all the encouragement I needed.

I mashed myself into the strong, hard shape of him. Droko was so phenomenally solid, I was sure he'd leave an impression against me like a boot would mark its tread on the soft bank of a river. And me? Well, I might have some grit, but underneath all that, I was pliant.

Our breath mingled, and he made that orcish whuffing noise. Cautious. In the pit of his throat. And then he

shuddered like a wagon crossing a rut. Yes, my human senses were dull compared to his, but even I could tell that the
places where we came together were utterly sublime. My
breath to his. My lips to his. My tongue to—

"Archie," he said sadly as he took a step back—I got goose-
flesh all over from the way he formed the word around his
tusks. "It can't be."

"But it can." I steeled myself and plowed ahead. "There's
a way out of these caves—a way none of the guards know
about." And while I'd never be able to cram him through the
narrow gap that led to my escape route, Dreadforge would
take care of that soon enough. I caught his arm and tried to
tug him toward the door. It was like dragging on a mountain.
"While everyone's busy putting together the fake tomb—"

"I'm sorry." Droko eased my hand from his forearm, holding it as if he was worried he'd squeeze too hard and hear
bones crunch. "Maybe, in another life, I could have gone
with you. But I have an obligation to my family. And if I
did manage to escape, retribution would rain down like—"

As if on cue, a massive peel of thunder boomed through
the caverns.

"You see?" Droko gave a joyless laugh as he glanced up at
the cave ceiling. "Even the skies are conspiring to keep me
on the unlikely path I've laid out for myself. I told Ul-Rott
rain would come for Taruut's funeral. And the heavens have
made me an honest man."

The sound of distant plinks and plunks filtered in as the
sudden downpour seeped into the caves. Against all odds,
they also filled my heart with hope. "Droko…what are the
chances it just so happened to rain exactly when you said it
would?"

"Unlikely or not, it's a coincidence. Nothing more."

"You're sure?"

"Positive. I'm as much a shaman as you are an orc. So, if you've found a way out, you should take it. In fact, I command you to go. While everyone is distracted with the funeral—"

"And leave you here alone? Unthinkable."

"Well. I suppose I'll always have Crespash."

I didn't have the heart to tell Droko that if I went, his goblin was sure to follow. I didn't need to. It was written all over my face...or whatever the scent equivalent might be. He smiled joylessly and said, "There's no sense in sending three soldiers into a losing battle when one will do. Crespash is a pain in the arse anyway, and I'll be fine without my food taster—Gorgul won't let anyone poison me. He's got too much to lose."

Gorgul. The mere sound of his name made my fingers itch to aim Dreadforge at something other than a cave wall. I might not be strong enough to swing it as high as his heart... but I could at least lop off a leg. "How did that wretched orc figure out you couldn't shaman? Is Crespash so bitter he would sell you out even if it meant he'd go down right along with you?"

Droko gave his head a single, ponderous shake. "The goblin's hatred runs deep. But he would never risk his own skin for the sake of revenge. He's a survivor."

Just like me. "Then how did Gorgul find out?"

"Does it matter? The ivories are cast." Up close like this, Droko felt so impossibly huge. A great hulk of an orc who could stand up to anything. And yet, his expression was so resigned, so profoundly sad, that it pained me to even look at him.

I've heard talk of heartache before. Nothing sadder than a

bedboy who actually believed it when a paying man called him special. Always figured I was too much of a realist to fall in love—that maybe I was just born without the sort of feelings that left those sorry boys pining away at the window for someone who never intended to come back for them.

Maybe I'd even *prided* myself in keeping my heart so untouchable.

And maybe that really had been the smart thing to do. Because here, now, faced with the thought of never seeing Droko again...it felt like the beating muscle had been ripped right out of my chest.

"Please." I knuckled the sting from my eyes, stretched up on tiptoe, and cupped his strong orcish face in my hands. "Don't send me away."

Droko stiffened, and I wondered if maybe I'd only succeeded in firming up his resolve....

Until he hitched me up by the armpits, swung me around, and pinned me to the wall.

19

DROKO

Archie.

His sweet human scent was rubbing off all over me, but I just couldn't stop myself. The taste of his breath scudding over my palate, the sweep of that agile tongue—

The memory of it sliding across the sensitive tip of my cock....

I shoved him against the wall. He was so light I could pin him there with hardly a thought, yet so limber that even through my rigid leathers, the feel of his thighs wrapping around my waist was enough to drive the breath right out of me.

If I'd been worried for him, maybe I could have stopped myself. But Archie had found a way out—he would soon be free—so it didn't matter if he was covered in my scent. Maybe it would even help him get away, masking his exotic musk beneath the more common smell of orc. A thin excuse. But I was desperate to believe it.

I shoved our mouths together, needing to smell him, taste him—to bathe in the human otherness of Archie's scent.

Orcs don't kiss, not on the mouth. Too many clashing tusks. But Archie's mouth fit against with mine as though they were made for one another.

He gasped. It landed like water on parched earth. I slid my hands beneath his shirt to make him do it again. The feel of his hot, smooth skin—so soft—the dip of his spine, the rippling of his muscles as he shivered beneath my touch....

I'd thought to wring some choice sounds out of him, but now I was the one biting back a moan.

I wanted more. Wanted to wrap my arms around him. To taste every inch, to explore the delicious depths of his humanness. To let his scent sink into me, to force it into my pores until I was so full of him that even once he was gone, he would still be a part of me.

I worked my hands lower and cupped his sweet, rounded arse in two firm handfuls. He arched his back, pushing his hips against mine as his breathing shifted into something ragged and unsteady. The scent of human arousal filled my senses as I shifted his body to grind his crotch against my lower belly.

"Droko...please," he breathed against my mouth, and I rolled my hips so the friction found him right between his spread legs. The scent of arousal intensified. And then he threw back his head and bared his pale, slender neck.

Whatever scant control I might've still possessed immediately shattered as my cock strained hard against my breeches.

I'd hooked a thumb into his waistband and was nigh ready to tear his clothes from his body when he said, "Please...come with me. I can't lose you."

The reality of what we were doing reared its head—the

danger, the futility—and I couldn't go on. My hands dropped to my sides, numb...and Archie slid down until his feet touched the floor.

Voice rough, I said, "You don't know what you're asking—"

"The hell I don't. How long will you play this crazy game, constantly worrying you'll be found out? The odds are against you, and eventually, you're gonna lose."

"But my clan—"

"I don't give the even the slightest damn about your clan. They sacrificed you to save their own hides. And as far as I'm concerned, they can find some other scapegoat to take your place."

He was right, of course. But I couldn't go. I might not have chosen this burden, but it was still mine. Walking away from it was...unthinkable.

"Take a chance," he said softly. "You're more than your clan, Droko. Be your own person."

When Archie reached up to cup my jaw, I flinched. Not because I was worried about his scent—I was covered in it already—but because I wasn't strong enough to do what he asked. I took a step back and his face fell.

"This is who I am," I said regretfully. "And I could no sooner set aside this responsibility than cut off my own—"

"Shh!" Archie jabbed a finger toward something just over my left shoulder and whispered, "Look at the tapestry. It's moving."

I figured I had jostled the old thing, but I turned and saw I was still a solid pace away. And the central figure, the tattered green orc, swayed like he was dodging a thrown spear. I remembered Gorgul discouraging me from looking at it too closely...and him telling me not to touch it.

I whisked the tapestry aside. Behind it, an eye-level hole the size of my fist had been hewn into the rock. Wind from the storm I'd "predicted" whistled through the tunnel beyond, and if I focused, I could hear the sound of distant rain.

The meditation room was supposed to be my sanctuary, or so I had believed—the only place in the caves where I had any sort of privacy. But instead, it was just a way for Gorgul to learn things to use against me. When I'd pried the teeth from the skull...when I'd taken pleasure with Archie.... None of my secrets had ever been secret at all.

"You know what this means," Archie said—and of course I did. It meant I was a fool. But that wasn't what Archie was trying to say. "It's especially satisfying to bend an enemy over a barrel when he thinks he's plugging *you*."

He peered through the hole, got his bearings, then let the tapestry fall back into place. His voice was low, but brimming with excitement, when he said, "Maybe you can't kill Gargle, but you can do one better. We'll feed him a fake plan so outrageous, he can't help but 'unveil' in front of everyone. Make him out to be a dumbass, and not only do you gain the upper hand—you discredit his word. Once his credibility is ruined, whatever he thinks he has on you is useless."

I wasn't convinced—and Archie wasn't done convincing me—but he held up a finger and pressed an ear to the tattered green orc. "Someone's coming," he whispered.

I took a measured breath and let the air play across my palate. Mostly, I smelled the room. Burning coals. Rotting wool. A lingering trace of incense. And, of course...I smelled Archie.

But underneath all of that, if I really reached, I picked up the scent of an orc.

Of Gorgul.

My arm ached with the need to thrust itself through the hole behind the crumbling tapestry, grab the traitor by the throat, and slam his head into the cave wall—and keep on slamming until the sound turned wet and sloppy. Killing him might only make things worse. Yet it would feel so damned good.

But I didn't move.

From the edge of my vision, I saw Archie's teeth glitter by the brazier's dim light, and I knew he was smiling. "Follow my lead," he said, barely a breath. Then, at a conversational level, he said, "Of *course* I can find Deathshade. There's enough of it in Taruut's apothecary to wipe out half the clan. All it takes is a few grains of the stuff, and *poof.* No more Ul-Rott."

Archie looked at me meaningfully, making a "go ahead" gesture he shielded from the spy hole with his body.

I'd never been any good at improvising. Too busy training to follow orders.

Archie gestured harder. I blanched.

"I can see you're hesitant," he said loudly, picking up the thread I couldn't seem to find. "Do you think a delayed reaction would be better? I could use Nightroot instead, and when the chieftain goes to sleep tonight, he won't wake up."

I was about to agree just to sound like I was calling the shots when I saw Archie give his head a subtle shake. "No," I blurted out.

He gave the "go on" motion again.

"Poison may be a coward's weapon," I said. The words felt wooden, halting...but I pushed ahead. "But I need to be there when it happens if I'm to seize power."

Archie's eyes sparkled with approval. "My Droko is sage, indeed. Deathshade it is. But how do we get him to swallow it?"

Well, that was easy. "The chieftain always takes the choicest offering. Lay out a plate of grubs for the ceremony and make sure you taint them just before you serve them so they're still wriggling. See that you feed Deathshade only to the fattest one. That's the grub Ul-Rott will pick."

"It almost sounds like you've done this before," Archie said playfully.

No. Thanks to my father, I simply knew how a leader would act. But since I was finally getting the hang of the lie, I said, "How do you think I got this far?" and was rewarded with an even broader smile. "Now, go, human. Prepare the meal. It will be the last one you ever make in this dark, stinking cave. Before the day is out, we'll paint the streets with the blood of any who oppose me and take our rightful place in the chieftain's hall."

20

ARCHIE

It was all an act. I knew it was. I'd orchestrated the whole thing myself.

And yet, when Droko spoke to me like that, all confident and commanding...well, I could hardly stop myself from jumping his bones right then and there. I hurried back to the kitchen to get ready for the chieftain's arrival with something *other* than dread filling my belly. It was still a queasy feeling, of course. But now it was tinged with anticipation.

Taruut once told me that a true orc is defined by his honor—though from what I gather, their opinion of right and wrong is pretty fluid. Never mind that Gargle was a backstabbing traitor. That sort of ambition was something all of them could wrap their heads around. But make him seem feeble, and apparently, he'd never recover.

Taruut would've been proud of our plan. He had a soft spot for cleverness.

Before he'd died, the old shaman had taught me about more than just orcish stubbornness. He'd schooled me on how to boil mallow to soothe a raw throat, and how to make a plaster of herbs and clay to cover an angry scrape. But instruct me in the art of poisoning? Of course not.

Taruut might've been batty...but he was no idiot.

The Deathshade didn't even exist, as far as I knew. I'd just made it up on the spot. Hopefully something in the larder would serve as a convincing substitute.

I sniffed through the culinary herbs, wishing I could borrow an orcish nose for the task–or even a goblin snout, for that matter. Crespash must have offloaded that horrid spider by now. But where he'd gone was anyone's guess.

After a few minutes of deliberation, I decided to go with the least pungent of the bunch. A poison that an orc could sniff out a mile away would hardly do its job, after all. I pried several jars from the back of the highest shelf, things covered in cobwebs that hadn't been opened in years. Some of the contents had petrified into a solid lump. Others were practically dust. I grabbed a handful of each and, one by one, ground them into a fine powder.

I was sneezing my head off by the time I finished. Maybe my fine spray of spittle would lend an extra oomph to my so-called poison. One could only hope.

Now it was just down to making a grub eat my concoction.

I went back to the larder and found a pot of the fattest grubs I could lay my hands on. Wincing, I plucked out a creature to get a closer look at it. The grub was the color of suet, with a translucent, segmented body, a pair of dark spots where eyes would someday develop, and two wriggling nubs for antennae. I thought of the chieftain crushing it between his teeth and my stomach heaved.

I quickly plucked a test grub from the bunch, a feisty thing the size of my thumb. It wriggled in my grasp, and I hastily dropped it into the powder, hoping that it would seize the opportunity to chow down. But instead, it just flopped about and covered itself in a fine coating of herbs. I quietly brushed it into the waste bucket.

What did grubs even eat? I poked around inside the pot and found my answer...and wished I hadn't. Evidently, they ate each other. Cringing, I plucked out another little cannibal and presented it with the powdered herbs. This time I set it on the edge of the plate...only to watch it roll in and coat itself.

I flicked it into the trash with its buddy.

I'll try anything once, but there's plenty of things I'd never imagined myself doing. Bathing in a geyser. Slicing through rock with a dwarvish sword. Kissing a man with tusks. But feeding a bloated white grub with the tip of a tiny spoon was definitely top of the list.

I watched in horrid fascination as its tiny mouthparts coaxed the herbal mixture into its gullet. And once the grub finished its meal, I carefully observed it to see if eating the mixture had any effects. Its movements were sluggish, and its antenna-nubs twitched as if in a trance. If my phony poison was actually toxic to bugs, then all my hard work would be for nothing. Orcs prefer their grubs alive and kicking–or writhing around, if you want to be technical about it–and no doubt serving the chieftain a dead grub would not only be suspicious. It would be an insult.

Did I have enough time to throw together another fake poison? Unlikely. A thrumming sound in a far-off corridor had the distinct pattern of hobnail boots, the very sort worn by Ul-Rott's guard. Maybe I'd be lucky and the grub would wait a few minutes to actually expire.

As if luck had ever been on my side.

I was scrabbling through the grub pot, searching for a fat enough understudy to take the place of the one I'd just accidentally poisoned for real, when I spied motion out of the corner of my eye.

Fattie had shaken off his stupor and was wriggling desperately around the plate.

The orcish footfalls grew louder. I had just enough time to add a handful of non-poisoned grubs to the dish, and a sprig of watercress for decoration. Hardly a meal fit for a chieftain, I realized, just as the orc reached the doorway.

Kof. All decked out in feathers and white face-paint.

"It's time, human," the orc barked at me. "Don't dawdle." He turned to go, then paused and added, "For some reason, Taruut always liked you. His spirit won't want to start without you."

With that, he scooped up the tray of grubs. But as he did, I noticed something alarming. Fattie now had a dark line of herbs running along the length of its translucent body.

"Wait," I called out, and Kof narrowed his single eye suspiciously. I cast about in desperation and spotted some rubyseed lingering in the mortar and pestle. "We can't serve the chieftain just any old grubs, can we?"

The spice was red—really red. Hopefully red enough to cover up a telltale dark line on a very portly grub.

I hastily flung the herb at the plate. Once I dusted it over the top, though, I realized I'd covered my tracks all too well.

The red spice powder made pink, wriggling cherries of my handiwork. Yes, the dark line was covered...but the smell of the subtle toxin I had so painstakingly created was entirely blotted out by the pungent stink of rubyseed.

Damn it—the grub was supposed to look just poisoned

enough to arouse suspicion, and now I'd gone and obscured all my hard work!

Kof grabbed the plate. "Hold on," I insisted, "a splash of wine—"

"Even you know better than to keep the chieftain waiting. Praise Ul-Rott."

I heaved a heavy sigh, and to Kof's retreating back, murmured, "Indeed. My ladle is his."

There hadn't been much time to prepare, but the honor guard had done an impressive job of turning an abandoned storeroom into a plausible tomb.

At least…I think they had. Kind of hard to tell with all the incense.

The irregular natural chamber was shrouded in a smoky haze, as if the walls were made of fog. The heavy incense burned like thick, cloying perfume and filled the chamber with a dizzying array of smells. Ul-Rott stood in the center, flanked by two enormous guards, their faces obscured by the smoke. The chieftain waved his hand in front of his face to clear away some of the smog so that he could see who had entered.

"Where's the blasted shaman boy?" he demanded of no one in particular. "Let's get this over with before I go blind."

I couldn't help but compare the impromptu crypt to the makeshift dwarven tomb I'd stumbled into before. They were nothing alike. While the dwarves slept their eternal sleep in a stately, quiet, dignified arrangement, the meditation chamber had been crammed with props. Among the chests and urns and statues, a half dozen wooden biers had been assembled. And on those slabs lay an assemblage of skeletons. Maybe not *whole* skeletons. I suspected that while there'd been a big selection of bones to choose from, they'd be a mishmash of various orcs and other unfortunates who'd ended up in the bone piles. But the rotting shrouds held them together well enough.

I had no attention to spare for the decorations, though. I was too busy watching my poison plan fall apart. I caught the eye of one of the honor guard and whispered, "Where's Gorgul?"

"How should I know?" he snapped, and I felt myself wither inside. Without Gorgul, there'd be nothing to show for my oh-so-clever plan but a spicy grub.

Meanwhile, Kof set the plate down directly within Ul-Rott's reach. The chieftain waved away the proffered food, his attention focused on something else entirely. "What's that writing scratched into the wall?" he asked Kof. A few members of the honor guard shifted subtly, wondering if they'd gone too far in their set dressing. Ul-Rott squinted. "Curses? Spells? Bah. This witchcraft makes my skin crawl."

"Who kens the ways of a shaman?" Kof said vaguely, and the chieftain grunted a non-reply.

Then Droko entered the room in full shaman regalia...and everyone went dead silent. No scuffed leather armor today. Instead, he wore a single deer hide slung low on his hips and a cloak with a spray of pheasant tails affixed to the collar. His hair had been freed from his topknot and braided with threads of gold. Most striking of all, though, was the big red-ochre hand print in the center of his chiseled bare chest.

Droko was no shaman. He'd told me so himself. He should have looked preposterous in shamanic adornments. But standing there so tall and proud and strong, he wasn't silly at all.

He was glorious.

He stepped forward and surveyed the room, his gaze taking in everything: the biers, the incense, the walls veiled in fog. He stood there for a moment *owning* that smoke-filled room, then gestured for a pair of Taruut's men to enter. I recognized them as one of the teams who'd carted the old man around in his sedan chair. In tandem, as always, they carried his shrouded form one final time to his resting place.

Droko brought with him a sense of calm assurance. His voice was low but clear when he spoke. "Taruut is here among us tonight," he said. "His spirit will be honored and remembered."

Ul-Rott watched him expectantly for a long moment, then narrowed his eyes and said, "That's it?"

"Now it's time for you to say a few words."

"Taruut is dead. He served the clan long...and well."

And...still, no Gorgul. Droko's gaze locked with mine and his eyes widened. To the chieftain, he said, "But surely there's a clever prediction of his that needs retelling—"

"The old man knew exactly what I thought—we didn't mince words. Let's face it, these ceremonies are for the living, not the dead. And Taruut was so old, we've all had plenty of time to say our goodbyes." With that blasé pronouncement, Ul-Rott waved aside a fresh cloud of incense and reached for a grub.

I'd been so worried the chieftain would grab the wrong one, I hadn't even considered he'd manage to do it while the target of our whole deception wasn't even here!

Ul-Rott plucked a wriggling morsel from the plate and gestured toward Taruut's bier. "And he'd certainly get a kick out of you being so extravagant with the rubyseed on his behalf."

Was that Fattie? I thought it was. So many places my cunning plan could fall apart, only to have it go awry because that stupid orc chose this particular moment to make himself scarce—

"Stop!" With the force of a boulder rolling off a cliff, Gorgul plowed into the room, striking the squirming grub from the Chieftain's hand.

If something like that had happened in the brothel, I can guarantee, most everyone would either be ducking under the table to avoid being hit by a random projectile, or pointing and laughing (if they simply couldn't resist.) But to these orcs? A swipe at their chieftain was no laughing matter.

Swords and spears whipped out faster than a paying man's dick eager for a quickie. The chieftain's men had a clear objective: keep Gorgul away from their leader. The honor guard of the shaman pointed their spears every which way since, irrational or not, Gorgul was one of their own. Kof waded through the pointiness and dragged his lieutenant away from the chieftain before anyone could do us the favor of running him through.

"Stand down," he barked at his men, then sent Gorgul reeling back with a well-placed shove, demanding, "What's this all about?"

Gorgul grabbed up Fattie and held him aloft so the light of the biggest brazier fell on its plump, squirming, spice-dusted body. "The grub you almost swallowed is poisoned!"

When Kof swung around and lined me up in the gaze of his single eye, I realized it was possible my plan might work out a bit too well. His grip on his spear tightened. I threw my hands up—would that stop him from running me through?—and said, "Poison? That's preposterous! It's covered in rubyseed, nothing more."

"I heard them spinning out their vile plan," Gargle insisted. "The new shaman and his pet human, planning to take over the clan. The poison is *inside* the grub."

All eyes locked on Fattie. Ul-Rott motioned one of his guards with a simple jerk of his chin, and the soldier pulled a skin from his belt and doused the grub with water. It flopped wetly in Gorgul's hand...with the dark line just showing through the translucent body.

"See?" Gorgul crowed triumphantly. "Its gullet is filled with—"

"Culinary herbs," I called out. "What, haven't you ever had a chicken stuffed with sage? Same thing!"

"Do you take the word of a *human*?" Gorgul snarled. "The shaman is clearly under his sway—they reek of each other!"

And then all eyes turned to me—and the pointy ends of all the weapons, too—just as the spasming grub leapt out of Gorgul's hand and landed with a splat directly between my feet.

Calm as you please, I picked up Fattie—stars above, he was *pulsating*—and looked Ul-Rott in the eye. "Culinary herbs, chieftain. Nothing more."

Then I popped the fat, wriggling creature into my mouth.

Let's just say it's a good thing I have no gag reflex whatsoever.

The grub had been daunting enough on the plate. Inside my mouth, it felt even bigger, the size of a soft-boiled quail egg. Same consistency too...if boiled eggs could freaking *move*. And, I realized, as Ul-Rott's shrewd gaze bore into me, that I'd never get away with swallowing the thing whole.

So...I bit.

It took every scrap of my self-control not to spew all over

the row of hobnailed boots that had closed in all around me. As to the taste, I had no idea. Couldn't get past the texture. And the *movement*. But one thing was for sure. The herbs I'd fed the grub before I plated him provided a most unwelcome grit.

I swallowed. Convulsively. And swallowed again. And only once I was positive I wouldn't hurl did I manage to say, "Delicious. An offering fit for a chieftain."

Ul-Rott waved for one of his trusted men to take up the plate. "You have the best nose—what do you make of this so-called poison?"

Gorgul shoved forward as the guard whuffed over the plate, but a sword leveled at his throat stopped him from interfering. The guard thumped his chest and said, "Nothing here but rubyseed powder, Ul-Rott the Spinecrusher."

Desperately, Gorgul said, "They fed the poison to a single grub...the one they knew you would take." Though it was obvious he could tell just how ridiculous he sounded as he said it.

A fact that the chieftain didn't overlook, either. "The one they just happened to know I would choose. The one the human himself just ate." He turned to Droko and said, "I'd keep an eye on your man. He's not in his right mind."

"The honor guard grieves for their fallen shaman," Droko said. I hadn't realized an orc could be diplomatic. "As do we all."

21

DROKO

"Making Gargle look unhinged was a stroke of utter genius." Archie rushed into the meditation room, grabbed the flask of wine he'd brought for me, and methodically downed the entire thing. He dried his lips with a swipe of his hand and said, "Er...which of us came up with the plan, anyway? Eh, doesn't matter. Not only did it put that bully in his place—it sent a clear message to his buddy-boys not to mess with the new shaman."

The grub trick sent a message, all right. But not the one Archie thought. A soldier is trained to spot his enemy's weakness. And by publicly proclaiming that Archie and I bore each other's scents, Gorgul had assured that whoever still wanted to strike at me could do so through my human.

"Archie...it's too dangerous for you to stay here." I did my best to keep my voice even and strong. "You have to leave."

He'd been beaming with excitement moments before, but now his face drained of color. "Wait...what?"

"You heard me. You can't stay. It's too risky. If one of Gorgul's followers decides to challenge me, he'll do it by hurting you."

"Hold on—you're saying I'm a *vulnerability*?"

Well...unfortunately, yes.

Archie squared his shoulders. "Who was the one who suggested using Gorgul's spy-hole against him, anyway? Oh yeah, now I remember. It was me."

I sighed.

"Who stood up to a bunch of musclebound brutes wielding pointy objects—armed with nothing but his good looks, I might add—to get said bully off your back? Also me."

"Archie...."

"And most important of all, who chewed and swallowed the world's fattest grub without so much as a hiccup?"

One thing I knew from observing my father was that until you truly proved yourself, when one enemy fell, another always rose up to take his place. "Gorgul is not the only honor guard to know I'm no shaman. The others are sure to find out."

"But it *rained*—"

"It doesn't matter. A true shaman would have found the crypt by tossing his ivories or consulting the spirits or...whatever. He wouldn't dress up a storage room with a pile of old bones. These men all know I failed. I can never win enough of their respect to keep us both alive."

"Especially when I'm so puny and weak." The bitterness in Archie's tone cut me like a blade...but he wasn't trying to hurt me. He had a point to make. "Don't forget, Droko—I knew Taruut. Knew him well. Not only was he too feeble to walk, but he was totally blind. He was so decrepit, he needed them to hold him over the bedpan while he pissed! Any one of the honor guard could have crushed his ribcage with nothing more than a gentle nudge—and gotten away with it by saying he'd fallen. If that's not vulnerable, I don't know what is."

"But he was a shaman—"

"Yeah. I noticed, what with all the incense and body paint and feathers. But here's the thing. Not once, in all the time I spent with him, did I ever see Taruut work any magic. He'd make a big show of reading his little teeth or going on about his cryptic dreams—"

So, I wasn't the only one plagued by nighttime disturbances. Something ill in the atmosphere, no doubt.

"—but Taruut's shamaning consisted of herbcraft, common sense, and a few vague predictions. Nothing more."

"It took years for Taruut to build up enough respect to protect him in his old age, Archie. Decades. And he was born to the Red Hand Clan. Not an outsider, like me."

When the mulish set of Archie's jaw told me that no amount of convincing on my part would change his mind, I strode to the far side of the meditation room, feathered neckpiece bobbing, and whisked aside the rotting tapestry to reveal the treacherous hole.

"Look at me, Archie." I gestured at the hole. "*This* is the problem. This is why you can't stay. There is no loyalty here for me. And there's no telling how long it will take me to earn it—if I ever do. And my happiness is not worth your life."

Archie's sky-colored eyes went to the hole, then found my gaze. Subdued, he said, "So…I make you happy?"

I took him in. Fierce. Defiant. Beautiful. "Of course you do."

He surged to his feet, rushing toward me. "Then I don't give a damn about the risk. Do you hear me? Because I'd rather be happy with you for a month—or a week, or even a day—than spend my life wondering how things could've been, if only I were brave enough to stick around."

Bravery would hardly protect him from death at the hands of my enemies. I tore a pouch from my belt—heavy, and cool to the touch—and thrust it into his grasp. "Stormsilver. Take it and go. At least then I'll know I've provided for you. You'll have a good life. The life you deserve."

Archie pulled out the stormsilver and let the empty pouch fall to the floor. The metal glinted dully by the light of the brazier, orange reflections swirling softly. "What use is some treasure if I've got no one to share it with? It's not the security I want, or wealth, or even whatever status might come with being the shaman's favorite. It's you."

"It's not *safe*." I jabbed a finger toward the spyhole.

Archie strode to the wall, chin tipped up, cheeks flushed. "I. Don't. Care."

He tried to prove his point by throwing the stormsilver away. It should have worked. While the lump of metal was certainly heavy, it was smaller than my fist. But its form was not as fixed as we thought, and when he thrust it into the circular hole, it somehow reshaped itself. It didn't fall through, nor did it bounce off. Instead, it ground into place with a stony snap that echoed through the chamber.

We stopped arguing and both looked at the thing, baffled.

And then the stormsilver crackled...and the floor shook.

One moment, it was a tickle through the soles of my sandals, and the next I was sure a cave-in would bury us both. A sparking fissure raced across the longest solid curve of the wall, the section that arced between the spyhole and the door. Light knifed through the crack, a sawtoothed zigzag that was far too regular to be natural. A light that was the color of fire.

It was a scene right out of my dreams. I half-expected to wake up before I was burned alive—except there was no heat, I realized. Only light.

A blinding orange light that brought me to my knees.

22

ARCHIE

Droko made a strangled sound and folded to the floor. I rushed over, terrified that a hunk of the ceiling had fallen in and brained him. It was all my fault. My own damn stubbornness had killed the man I loved....

Loved!

But there was no fallen rock. Or gore. Or splattered brain. Droko was unharmed...mostly. He knelt, stiff and unseeing, with his arms thrown wide, back arched. The vibrant gold flecks in his irises were now swirling like embers in a flaring campfire, and the painted hand on his chest shone in the amber light like fresh blood.

"Droko!" I shook him—or I tried to, anyhow. He was stiffer than the petrified dwarves—

Dwarves! Was this their work? It had to be. As I watched, the curved wall fragmented like the petals of a flower, then those petals slotted themselves neatly into the floor with a rasp of stone on stone. Taruut always said I was the key to everything. I didn't think he'd meant it literally! The workmanship I'd unlocked was so precise, it hardly looked like stone at all as it revealed a secret chamber.

A chamber I'd seen before—the amber room.

It had been striking enough by the glow of my lantern. But now it sparkled with a dazzling light. Small holes were drilled high in the ceiling, fitted with tiny mirrors. Sunlight bounced from the holes to the thick amber walls, sparkling so bright it forced me to blink away tears.

As the overhead light shifted, so did the sparkles. I couldn't quite say whether what I saw in Droko's eyes were the flecks he'd been born with or just the reflection of the dancing light. "Droko? Droko! Say something!"

The gold sparkles converged over each pupil, blinding him with a pair of radiant stars. Droko drew a deep breath...and spoke. "The Red Hand Clan shall be reborn in the fire of a new age, guided by the wisdom of its ancestors, and led by a son of the true sight."

His normally shivery-deep voice pealed through the amber room like thunder. Not just with volume, but with confidence.

It wasn't the blustery confidence of a chieftain...it was the knowing confidence of a shaman.

Droko's eyes flickered, and I realized that the sparkles hadn't blinded him at all. As figures of gilded light cascaded across the amber walls, Droko was reading them. I scuttled back to get out of his way, and as I did, I saw we weren't alone. The grinding walls had attracted some of the honor guard—and a few of the chieftain's men, as well. They'd all been pretty macho when they were pointing their weapons at me. But now, with the walls ablaze and the golden prophecy dancing all around them, they were singing another tune! Most of them cowered. Some made hasty gestures to ward off a curse. One of them actually pissed himself.

And in the face of it all, I stood my ground. Little ol' me. The weak and feeble human. I was patting myself on the back for being so brave when I realized Droko still had more to say.

"Seek the sign of the Hand, for it is not through blood that the clan is made strong, but through the convergence of hearts and minds. This is the time to unite, the time to stand as one...and the time to be made whole again."

The room was still. For a moment, no one stirred. Then, somewhere in the crowd, one of the bemused guards spoke up. "What's this sign of the Hand?"

"It's a *lie*," boomed a voice I knew all too well—just as Gorgul barreled into the amber room and backhanded me so hard I saw stars of my own. My ears rang, and the tang of copper flooded my mouth where my teeth cut into my cheek. Droko had been right: courage might be great, but all the bravery in the world won't protect a small, soft unarmed human from a gigantic raging orc.

But it wasn't actually me Gorgul was after. I'd simply been knocked aside for standing in his way.

It was Droko.

Kneeling. Bare-chested and vulnerable. Unarmed.

Defenseless.

His honor guard couldn't help, and neither could the chieftain's men. They'd all crowded against the far side of the room to get away from the so-called "witchcraft." And even if it would do any good to fling myself in front of Droko like a human shield, my head was ringing so hard I could barely see straight, let alone try and stop the attack.

Gorgul had no weapon, but it didn't matter. He seized

Droko by the throat. Humiliated rage contorted his features, and flecks of spit hit Droko's face as he bellowed, "You think you can come here and preach your lies? I will choke them from your foul body—"

I lurched toward them, blacked out for half a heartbeat, and sagged against the amber wall, useless. But Droko did even less. He hung there, making no attempt to pry Gorgul's hands off his neck. His arms hovered at his sides, spread wide. And his lips still moved as words of light whirled around him while Gorgul choked off his air supply.

The honor guard was useless. I was useless. And Droko was clearly so far gone in the grip of the prophecy he had no hope of defending himself.

As golden letters cascaded through the air all around me, bouncing off the amber, I banked off the wall and staggered toward Droko. I knew that even if I reached him in time, I was no match for an orc. *Any* orc. Especially a warrior in his prime. No doubt Gorgul would crush me. But at least I'd die knowing—

The handprint on Droko's chest flared as if it had been daubed in saltpeter and sparked by a flame. Gorgul jerked his head away from the flash, just as a lightning-fast figure cut through the cascade of golden letters.

Crespash.

The goblin flung himself from a crack in the wall—and he hadn't shown up at the party unarmed. The blade in his hand cut the very air with a loud *shing!*...followed by a stony crunch as Dreadforge buried its tip in the glowing amber floor.

I'd known Crespash was stronger than me. But I could barely lift the sword high enough to chip away a stairstep.

He'd swung it over his head in a mighty arc. And props to him—I wasn't even angry he'd found my sword. Even though his crazy swing had missed, at least his bold move had commanded Gorgul's attention.

Droko swayed on his knees as the traitor's hands slid from his throat, but he didn't collapse. His eyes were still spinning with gold.

I hovered there on the balls of my feet, trying to work out who Gorgul would lunge for next, Crespash or me—and if it was me, which way I should dodge. No doubt he'd love to rid the world of either of us.

As he wavered, one of the useless guardsmen declared, "The sign of the hand," and I felt the imprint of Gorgul's outspread fingers burning on my cheek. It was familiar. Not like an old friend. More like a tune you can't stop humming in the middle of the night when you should be getting some sleep. The new handprint was likely larger than the one I'd picked up back in the slaver's tents—the mark that caught the orcs' attention to begin with—but it had landed in the very same spot.

But this time, the handprint pulled at me, dragging my gaze to the painted red print on Droko's chest...directly over his heart.

Gorgul's eyes fell to the paint, then lit on the matching handprint he'd laid across my cheek. He opened his mouth to speak—to challenge Droko's vision, no doubt—and then opened his mouth wider. Wider. Impossibly wide, in a soundless, lopsided yawn, eyes huge...as his head slid apart in a diagonal slice from ear to jaw, as precise and sharp as the invisible seams in the walls around us.

Dreadforge hadn't missed, after all.

The top half of Gorgul's head hit the ground with a meaty thump, rocked in place a few times, and finally went still... just as his body collapsed.

23

DROKO

I'm told I had a vision.

To me, it felt more like a dream—like the chaotic night-mares that had plagued me since I first allowed myself to sleep in the geyser caves. But this time, I hadn't exactly been sleeping. And I'd spoken aloud of what I saw. So if that's what prognostication truly was, well then....

Vision was as good a word as any.

I just hoped it didn't happen again anytime soon.

I'd made an impression, that was for sure. My honor guard had been respectful before, but only as far as duty dictated. Now? They were terrified.

The only one who could even bring himself to look at me was Kof. Maybe, to his single eye, I was only half as fright-ening. And while he stank of fear as much as all the rest of them, at least he forced himself to do his job.

He genuflected low and said, "The chieftain has been summoned and the slaves are secure."

Neither Crespash nor Archie would be happy about their confinement, but the guardsmen were all jumpy, and I couldn't risk either of my slaves ending up on the wrong side of a blade. "Get up," I told Kof. I needed another set of eyes—or at least a single intelligent one—to puzzle through what the dwarves had hidden all those years ago.

The amber walls glowed with eldritch light that shifted and danced. Something aboveground dappled the daylight streaming in through the small shafts—a cloud, perhaps, or maybe a branch. I kept my eyes firmly on the floor, worried that the dancing light would provoke another "vision." A queer tingle in the back of my neck that preceded the prior episode was absent. But I didn't want to take any chances.

The chamber was natural. The center had been a tree, once. A massive tree as wide as a hut. At some point deep in the past, its own sap had overtaken it and the core had rotted away, leaving this hollow. Maybe it then sunk into the cliffside, or maybe the rock had formed around it. Either way, it had been eons in the making—and then worked with dwarvish craftsmanship to house the bones of the shamans.

The work of dwarves is so cunning that the ignorant take it for sorcery. But the fact that I knew it for what it was—staggeringly complex and unerringly precise mechanics—didn't tarnish my opinion of the crypt in the least.

The far side of the chamber had slid open to reveal the final resting place of the Red Hand Clan's shamans—a single galley. Kof and I moved into the dark hall, him raising a lantern to try and see what we'd discovered.

A dozen biers flanked the long, narrow space, half of them empty, the other half home to dead shamans. The mummified remains had been undisturbed inside either of our lifetimes, and their elaborate ceremonial garb had fallen to rot.

Kof made a fist and blew into it like he was staving off

cold—a ward against evil I recognized from my father's superstitious kobold chambermaid—but he stuck by my side, which was what mattered most.

It wasn't the bodies that held my attention...but the writing on the wall.

I'd always been criticized for my interest in words and letters. But the figures here were archaic and difficult to ken, even for me—at least until I got my bearings and was able to discern one word, then another...and their meaning unfolded.

A faithful server shall accompany the shaman into the afterlife,
Steadfast until the end,
May they be at peace in the halls of the ancestors,
And together shall they remain.

It was then I saw that the biers weren't solid stone. Each platform was more like a table, with a narrow vault hollowed out beneath—just the right size for a second body.

Slotted in below every interred shaman was the corpse of a slave. Bound. Festooned with nonsense mystical charms. Likely buried alive.

With mounting panic, I realized that Taruut kept no slaves, save one.

Archie.

Approaching footsteps echoed through the caves. Not the slap of the sandals worn by my honor guard, but the stomp of hobnailed boots. Above that, Ul-Rott's annoyed tones carried across loud and clear. "If this turns out to be another false alarm, I'll have you all castrated!"

"Shutter the lantern," I whispered, and Kof hurried to comply.

"Shaman!" the chieftain called out. "What's all this I hear

about...?" His voice trailed off as I stepped out of the true crypt. Ul-Rott stood in the newly exposed amber room, mouth agape. A huge sword protruded from the floor and Gorgul's corpse was sprawled at his feet, but he took no notice, looking from one wall to the other as glowing figures danced across the surface. The overhead light was fading now, and the sparkling letters were dim and erratic. But even faded, they painted a dramatic scene.

Ul-Rott planted his hands on his hips and said, "What is this curse'd place?"

"It's the tomb of the shamans, great Spinecrusher." I would have added a respectful thump, but the red ochre handprint on my chest burned like a brand.

Ul-Rott grunted, then narrowed his eyes. "If that's so, then why did we park Taruut's body somewhere else?"

I knew chieftains. I knew how they thought, but most importantly, I knew how they felt: always bristling for a challenge. Appeasing the ego of a chieftain was a balancing act. And if I answered wrong, Ul-Rott would not be impressed by our find, but rather take offense at the lie we'd told to get here.

It was a lose-lose proposition. Either he'd think me an idiot for not finding the original tomb sooner, or deem me untrustworthy for creating a fake. But I had to give him *some* explanation. I hesitated...then saw him surreptitiously blow into his fist.

"It was foretold," I said simply.

Ul-Rott narrowed his eyes. He glanced down at Gorgul's corpse. "And this one?"

"Driven mad by the death of his leader. As you saw when he struck the grub from your hand."

Ul-Rott squinted at the golden letters flowing across the walls. I'd read prophecy in those words of light, but now I saw nothing but sparkles. What did Ul-Rott see there—a pronouncement that would lead Archie to his death? I was glad for the copper smell of blood in the air. Its tang would cover up my sour nerves. But the longer Ul-Rott paused, the more likely it was he'd see through my confident act and we'd all be lost....

Until finally he flexed his fingers as if he wished to blow into them again and shuddered. "Foretold? Hmph. As you say, Droko. Do you need me to speak more words, or can you handle the final interment yourself?"

He'd used my name. I was stunned. I gathered my wits and said, "I have everything under control."

The chieftain's gaze returned to what remained of Gorgul. "And what of this one? Will you send him to the pyre or leave him for the wolves? Your man, your choice."

"Actually...." the notion took hold before I had time to think it through, but I let the momentum carry me. "He was Taruut's man. And his madness was a testament to how bonded they were. He will rest in the tomb with his shaman, and make up for his insults by serving Taruut in the afterlife."

"If you put stock in that sort of thing," Ul-Rott muttered, then considered the body. "Taken down by a mere goblin, the men tell me. Better to weed him out now before he fails you in battle."

I looked up sharply. "Battle?"

"Of course. What good is a shaman built like an iron forge if I can't parade him around in front of my enemies? You can carry that blade over there. No one else is willing to touch the thing, but it would be a shame for such a stout weapon

to go to waste. You'll need to learn to ride a horse, though."
He adjusted his breeches and added, "I hope your choad is
up to it."

"And what of my slave?" My thoughts were of Crespash,
of course, who'd been hauled off by the honor guard after
saving my life.

But Ul-Rott had a different slave in mind. "What you do
with the human is your concern. Considering the big show
the two of you put on here, spending your seed on him obviously hasn't done your sorcery any harm."

Once Ul-Rott was gone, I ordered my men to bundle
Gorgul into the vault, then fetch Taruut's body. I couldn't
say for sure which guards had been poisoned by Gorgul's
words and which had always been loyal to me. But giving the
lieutenant the dignity of burial with his master was bound
to win back a few hearts.

Plus, now that my guardsmen had seen me spew some
"prophecy," they wouldn't dare stand against me.

Kof was the only one who'd willingly come within arm's
length—and that was something of a relief. Until he surprised me by saying, "It shouldn't be Gorgul in that crypt."

"Hold your tongue," I snapped.

But I'd told the captain to be blunt with me, and he was
determined to speak his mind. "Gorgul may have served as
Taruut's guard, but he never truly belonged to the shaman."

"Kof...." If I had to make an example of him, I would. Anything it took to protect Archie.

"You saw the writing on the wall," Kof said. "You read it
to me yourself. *A faithful companion.* Does that sound like
Gorgul to you?"

"Regardless of what we thought of Gorgul, he served

Taruut much longer than Archie."

Kof's scarred brow furrowed. "The slave? I would never suggest the human deserved the honor."

Then what on earth was he going on about?

He added, "If anyone here should accompany the shaman, it's me."

After the grub debacle, back when I'd told the chieftain that the honor guard was mourning their fallen shaman, I'd simply been uttering the sort of meaningless words men bandy about when they need to save face. It hadn't occurred to me that some of the guards might actually be grieving.

Kof said, "I've been here ever since I can remember. Before this happened," he gestured to his massive scar, "there's nothing. Like I didn't exist. I was young, but not that young. They say a wild animal...." He shuddered and stared off into the distance of his own murky past. "But Taruut...him, I remember, clear and true. He didn't just heal me. Once my wounds scarred over, he kept me close. Taught me things. Promoted me to his honor guard, even though the others said I was nowhere near bloodthirsty enough to protect him."

He fell into another of his strange silences. But when I stopped myself from interrupting it, I was rewarded with more.

"I never left these caves after that. I didn't need to. Taruut said everything was exactly as it should be. Made me his captain, even though nobody understood why. But Taruut... he always saw what others couldn't."

So it seemed. I wished I'd had the chance to meet the old man—although he probably would have seen right through my lies. "Taruut was a powerful shaman. He doesn't need your help to navigate the afterlife. Continue to serve him by serving me."

"You are the shaman," Kof said automatically. But when he took a moment to consider my words, maybe he truly was convinced. "I suppose I can't deny Taruut the chance to knock Gorgul down a peg."

24

DROKO

The burning handprint on my chest had subsided to a dull ache by the time I finally headed back to my sleeping quarters to shed myself of feathers and paint, tie my hair up, and lay down my weary body. Taruut's litter was gone now. But the broad cushion from the meditation room had been dragged in, taking up most of the space. And sprawled on that cushion...was Archie.

Not dead. Not even harmed.

Just sleeping.

He smelled of sulfur, as if he'd scrubbed off the violence of the day in the spout of the Great Whale. But the handprint that blazed on his pale cheek couldn't be sloughed off so easily. I tossed my feathered cloak over a nearby chest and knelt on the floor beside him. When I ghosted my fingertips across the angry red mark, the matching print on my chest prickled...just as Archie's eyes, the color of sky, fluttered open.

"Aren't you worried about putting your scent on me?" he said with a sleepy smile.

I traced the thumb's contour, which stretched across the

crest of his cheekbone. "We bear the same mark. So, it's common knowledge now that you are mine...and I am yours."

He crooked an eyebrow. "Maybe orcs and humans aren't so different after all. You can get away with pretty much anything...once you prove you're a badass. Dare I ask—are you still bent on sending me away? Or now that we belong to each other, do I get a reprieve?"

"How much more plainly can I say it?"

"Humor me," he said teasingly.

I'd never been much for pretty words, but I did my best. "A slave is his master's property, but you're not property to me. In fact, you've never been mine to command. I think of you like a hawk that perches by a man's campsite, or a fox who deigns to accept a bit of meat...a wild, untamed thing who only stays with me because it pleases you to do so. Though I hope you'll stick around."

"Of *course*, it pleases me to stay. It pleases me very much." Archie grabbed my hand, then turned to brush his lips across my palm. My breath caught. When he spoke again, the light, bantering tone was gone. "But back there in the amber room.... What came over you?"

"There's old magic in these caves—"

"Maybe so. And yet, it didn't send the other orcs to their knees. It drew no prophecy from anyone else. Only you."

In my heart, I was still a soldier. But if the clan truly thought I was their shaman, then that would need to be enough.

Archie noticed my eyes raking the enticing curve of his hip. He smiled into my palm and said, "Should we adjourn to the private meditation room? One of the walls is missing now—but I don't think we'll be disturbed."

"We can stay right where we are. If my scent is on you, and yours on me, no one would dare challenge it. Not after what happened in the crypt."

Archie tugged at my wrist, encouraging me to join him on the cushion. It wasn't quite big enough for both of us, but if I braced one foot on the floor, I could manage to spread out beside him. Archie prodded the handprint on my chest. "Does it hurt?" he asked as his fingers traced the outline of the hand.

"Some," I admitted.

"Good. Because I want to make an impression." Before I knew it, he'd flipped me onto my back and straddled my thighs, pinning my arms to my sides, with his mouth hovering just above my heart. "I want to make sure you *feel* this."

Oh, I felt it, all right. But when his hot breath played across the handprint...it was anything *but* painful. He gripped my wrists tight—for a human—and while I could shed him by simply standing up, I was intrigued by the deeper meaning. Archie wanted me. And he would take what he wanted.

His breath hissed over my scorched chest and he ground against my thickening cock. "Da-yum. Your hard-on's practically lifting me off your lap."

"This is what you do to me."

The tips of his ears went pink. "Yes. Well. I'm told there's a way I could actually take it—something called Easewater—"

"I've heard of this."

"—but with all the plotting and scheming going on, I haven't had the chance to brew a batch myself."

"Archie." I cupped his tuskless face and tilted his chin so he was looking me in the eye. "If I am yours, and you are mine, then we have plenty of time for Easewater. There are so many things I want to do with you, we'll never get through them all in a single night. And it would be a shame to even attempt it, when I want to cherish every touch and taste."

His eyes flicked to the side.

"What is it?" I asked.

"It's just that I've *done* all the things. Many times over, in fact, with countless men—whether I wanted to or not." Archie swallowed hard, and his scent tinged with saline. "But I can't say I've ever been cherished."

"Then we'd better do this right." I gentled him off of me and headed over to the shelves of bones and baubles that lined the chamber. Nothing was labeled. But I'd conditioned enough blades with rocknut oil to know the smell anywhere.

I turned and let my hide kilt drop to the floor.

Archie stood and faced me. His eyes went to my cock, hanging heavy and dark, thick with arousal. "Actually..." he said. "Maybe it *is* worth taking a brief respite to whip up that potion—"

I unstoppered the oil, gave it a sniff just to be sure, then pressed the phial into his hands. "One step at a time. When I couple with you, I want it to be good. But I won't know how it's supposed to be unless I've felt it for myself."

Archie's brow furrowed. "Hold up. You want *me*...to top *you?*"

"You just said you've done all the things."

"Well, sure. I just thought...I mean, you're so...."

Had I ever before seen him at a loss for words? "Since this is all new to me."

"Being with a human," he clarified. "Or did you mean being with a man?"

"Being with anyone."

Archie's mouth worked and nothing came out. But eventually, he managed, "You're a virgin?"

I shrugged. "I am untouched...aside from that thing you did with your tongue, obviously."

Archie sat down hard on the cushion. "Well. I see."

"I was to be wed. But my betrothed was given to someone else."

"Oh." He turned the bottle around in his hands. "I'm so sorry."

Strangely enough, I realized *I* wasn't. I crouched beside Archie, which put my face level with his. I coaxed his lips toward mine. He moaned into my mouth as I deepened the kiss. I could feel his hands shaking as he pushed the phial of rocknut oil aside and wrapped his arms around my neck. I pulled him closer still, pressing our bodies together and feeling the warmth of him against my bare skin. He wore far too many clothes now, and yet the barrier of the fabric between us only heightened my anticipation.

With one hand, I reached down and slipped a hand between his thighs, stroking him through his tight breeches as we kissed. Archie's hips jerked forward, and he gasped into my mouth. "You don't kiss like a virgin."

"And you," I murmured against his lips. "You don't kiss like a jaded man who's done it countless times before."

Archie shifted his hips as his cock strained his breeches. "True, I've had my fair share of sex. But, kissing? That's reserved for someone special."

His tongue skimmed my lower lip, and I shivered. I wanted more. I wanted to touch him, kiss him, taste him—to feel him, in every way possible.

I cupped him between the legs and found a hardness that

startled me…mainly because it was most definitely not an erection.

"Sorry 'bout that." Archie pulled a bone-handled dagger from his breeches and set it aside. "I thought some protection was in order."

"You don't need to hide it. I will say you are allowed to carry a blade—and no one will dare contradict me."

"Have I mentioned how alluring it is when you're not second-guessing yourself?"

I answered with an amused huff and slid my hand up the inside of his thigh, finding my prize and reveling in the feel of his arousal. Orc cocks stiffen when the time comes to couple, but apparently, human cocks grow. I gasped at the sensation of his hardness prodding against my hand, much bigger than I'd anticipated. If orcs were proportioned like that, our partners would never walk again.

As I learned the shape of his cock, it grew bigger still. "I need to see," I gasped, pulling from our kiss.

"What a relief…I'm a heartbeat away from busting out of my new pants!" Archie's human shirt was a confounding series of lacings and tucks, but thankfully, his breeches were straightforward. While he struggled to free himself from his shirt, I tugged the breeches around his knees. His hard cock bobbed free, ruddy and smooth—and fragrant with human musk. "It's…bigger than I expected."

"I'm not quite sure if that's a compliment or a—oh yeah, sweet mercy, yes…."

I wanted to sniff, to savor—but I also wanted to make him tremble with pleasure. There'd be time to revel in all the new scents later. Right now I focused on sucking his pretty human cock.

I went at him mercilessly—like so many of my bunkmates claimed they'd been pleasured, though probably it was all just a brag they'd made up, given how the only thing we did outside the longhouse was wade into skirmishes. Archie seemed to enjoy it, if the broken sounds coming out of his throat were any sign. Or the way he scrabbled at my head.

My topknot came loose. Archie grabbed a hank of hair with one hand and a tusk with the other, and pumped into my mouth like his life depended on it. I relished his taste, salty and musky with just a hint of sweet bitterness, as his cockhead butted my throat.

Archie's knees locked as he closed in on the edge. I could feel his sack tighten, and I knew he was about to spill his seed. But before he could, I pulled away.

He looked at me, panting hard, with an incredulous mix of confusion and desperation. "Why did you stop?"

I found the phial of oil that had rolled onto the floor and pressed it into his hand. "I want to feel you inside me."

Cheeks flushed, he shoved the rest of the way out of his breeches. "Lie back," he said, voice husky, and I spread myself on the ridiculous cushion. He let out a shuddering breath as he slicked his fingers with oil while his gaze roamed my body. "I'd ask you to tell me if I'm hurting you, but I suspect a strapping, young orc hardly knows the meaning of the word."

"Then I'll be sure to let you know when something feels good."

Archie's eyes sparkled. "I think I can figure that out—since I *have* done this a time or two. But don't worry. I'll do my best to teach you everything I've picked up along the way."

He spread my legs wide and probed me with oiled fingers—taking too much care, I suspected, though I didn't correct him. I was more concerned about learning how humans touched each other so that when the time came, I didn't damage the fierce, fragile wild creature that insisted on staying by my side simply because it pleased him to do so.

Once I was slickened, Archie pushed my knee into my chest and prodded my arse with his cock. It didn't just seem proportionally large anymore, and human cockheads were less tapered than an orc's. I grunted as the bluntness of his tip strained against my tightness. Archie paused and said, "We don't have to."

"No. But I want to."

Hovering over me, he reached down to stroke my cheek. "Don't worry, my sweet shaman. I'll make it good for you."

It already was. Feeling his silken thighs against mine, basking in the scent of his human arousal, gazing into his sky-colored eyes...I'd never felt anything better. And the sting in my arse was quickly forgotten when the glide of the oil took over and Archie flexed his nimble hips just so. He fucked me deliberately, shifting his angle with every few thrusts, watching my face as if waiting for—

Oh.

Satisfaction curved the corner of his mouth. "That's it—right? The sweet spot." He thrust again, rubbing up against something inside me, and an indescribable flood of pleasure throbbed through my body, lighting me up like the amber room, heightening the sensation of everything at once...but mostly my aching cock.

"You clenched so hard I nearly lost it." Archie's color was high and his words came on a ragged breath. "But I owe it a few good prods at least...if only to see the look on your face, and know I've put that look there."

A bead of arousal dropped to my belly from the tip of my own cock as Archie thrust, and thrust again. Sweat glistened on his brow in the steamy heat of the caves, and soon his limbs with their silken skin were sliding against mine.

He bent forward to press his lips to the throbbing handprint on my chest—which now felt more like pleasure than pain—and trapped my cock between us.

Orcs don't perspire like humans do. Archie's scent was like nectar on my palate, heady and intoxicating. And the slick of his smooth belly, damp with sweat against my shaft, soon had me reeling toward my peak. I was just as helpless as I'd been in the amber room when the prophecy took me. But this joining with Archie didn't obliterate me....

It made me whole.

Strands of hot seed flooded between us as orgasm surged through me. My arse was ready for his cock now—no, it was eager—and he fucked me hard, bumping the place deep inside that had me seeing stars—in the best possible way. Archie's thrusts grew wild, even frantic, until his own peak overtook him. With a guttural sound, he clenched all over, and the salt of his human spend mingled with my musk.

Levered up on his elbows to gaze into my eyes, Archie went very still—aside from his breathy panting, and the tremble of exertion in his thighs. His cock was starting to soften and return to its usual unassuming posture. But neither of us wanted this first joining to be over just yet.

Even if it wouldn't be the last.

With a regretful sigh, Archie eventually pulled out. I lowered my knee, and he stretched out beside me. Somehow, we both fit on the cushion now. Probably because he was mostly draped over my chest with a leg slung across my thighs.

I turned my head to gaze at my human lover as he trailed absent patterns through the sticky seed on my belly, while somewhere deep within the cave, the Great Whale geysered its own spume. The cheek bearing the red handprint was facing away from me, but still, I felt its echo in my chest.

This wasn't how I expected my first time to be, I decided. Not at all. I'd expected to be in a normal house. With a normal wife. And certainly to be burying my cock instead of sheathing one.

But when I basked in the smooth, pale, lightly freckled angle of Archie's cheek and jaw, the wisp of red fur on his upper lip and chin, the expressive arch of russet brown eyebrows over his sky-colored eyes...I could scarcely recall what Farya even looked like.

And I certainly wasn't thinking of her when I cupped Archie's face in my hand and drew his sweet lips to mine.

25

ARCHIE

I might not have mastered the art of sleeping with one eye open, but my time in the brothels made me a light sleeper, for sure. Bedboys and wenches have nimble hands. And if you ever do manage to set a coin or two aside, they'll gladly relieve you of your hard-earned pennies while you're visiting dreamland. So, when I heard the familiar slap of sandal on stone, I flinched awake immediately.

Gorgul was dead. Intellectually, I knew it. I'd seen the top of his head slide off. But sleep-woozy me was positive my nemesis had finally come to put an end to me after all. I jerked up from the cushion, making Droko grunt in his sleep as I cast around for the knife and cursed myself for letting my guard down.

The brazier had burned low and the chamber was filled with shadows. But the hulking figure that had slipped into the room made no move to throttle me. It simply set a tray down among the clutter on the nearest semi-clear surface.

"Kof?"

The huge orc turned to line me up in his good eye. I

suddenly felt profoundly naked, but he didn't act like anything was amiss. Or even particularly remarkable.

Orcish ways were gonna take some getting used to.

Kof knelt under Droko's sleepy gaze. "I told you Taruut encouraged me to learn cookery. Since the bearer of the prophecy could hardly be expected to do such menial work, I figured I might as well handle it. That way I'll know for sure nobody's been poisoned."

"That's probably for the best," Droko rumbled. "Archie's cooking keeps getting worse. Now he doesn't even need a toxic herb to poison someone with it."

"Hey," I complained automatically...though he wasn't wrong. Even I could smell that the orc knew what he was doing at the hearth.

"This doesn't relieve you of your guard duties," Droko told Kof. "You're still the captain."

Kof puffed up, just a little, as he rose to his feet—but it was obvious the order pleased him. "As you wish, Droko the Starry-Eyed."

The look on Droko's face was priceless. "I can't deny those flecks in his irises are enchanting," I said, "But Droko the Starry-Eyed is quite a mouthful. How about Droko the Mystic?"

"If you must," Droko said with infinite patience.

Kof nodded, then turned to go, adding, "Oh, and I was sure to heap on plenty of those grubs the human likes."

Delightful.

"Mystic," Droko grumbled, once Kof was gone. "I preferred Sage."

While Droko might not have put much stock in esoteric matters, he hadn't seen the way the prophecy took him. But he was nothing if not pragmatic, so no doubt he'd come around to the idea eventually.

And speaking of pragmatic.... Good thing I was used to flicking weevils off my bread. I shoved the bugs aside and helped myself to what was underneath. Stewed meat of some kind, with something starchy, and something green. Whatever it was, it was well seasoned, so I figured I should stop trying to figure out what exactly it might be and simply eat my fill.

Droko was happy enough to shovel down all the grubs. I'd have to do my best not to think about it the next time I kissed him. And then my heart got all soppy over the thought of a *next time*. Because with a paying man, that sort of thing is never a given.

Though I couldn't help but remark, "Never mind that they're moving...." I shuddered. "The way they just pop between your teeth."

"If they're young enough, you don't even need teeth. Crespash loves 'em."

Crespash.

I'd been so wrapped up in Droko that I hadn't given a thought to the goblin. Not gonna lie, Crespash freaked me out. And when I saw him barrel into the amber room with that sword in his gangly arms, I'd thought for sure Droko was a goner. But instead of taking his revenge on his master... he'd saved Droko's life.

I thought back to the annoying peddler's words: *I could never be a slave. No matter how finely gilded the cage.* Kof hadn't referred to me as a slave. He'd called me the *Bearer of the Prophecy*—which had a pretty good ring to it, if I did say so myself.

Crespash, however, hadn't fared quite so well after the craziness in the amber room. He'd been hauled off by a pair of burly orcish guards.

"You need to help him," I said.

Droko's ponderous brow furrowed. "Crespash? Help him what?"

For someone so smart, he was incredibly dense when he wanted to be. "Help him escape so he can start a new life."

"Crespash is a slave. And for good reason. He's been a slave longer than I've been alive."

Droko seemed to consider the matter closed, but it was bugging me. If Crespash had found the sword I had so "cleverly" hidden, then it made sense that he'd found the escape route I'd been carving, too. He'd had an out. And he hadn't taken it.

Because he cared about Droko.

Droko had stood to eat. I squared myself up in front of him, eye-level with the handprint branded on his chest. Some of the red had settled out, and now it was more of a green-tinged rust. When I fit my hand over it, his breath hissed through his teeth. "Orcs have a highly developed sense of fairness, I've observed, and they put a lot of stock in doing what they feel is right. So, consider this. While you were on your knees with stars swirling through your eyes, Crespash could've easily lopped off your head right along with Gorgul's. But he didn't. He saved you."

Droko heaved a sigh. "Freeing slaves is not the orcish way." As he said this, he took in the chamber bedecked in bones and furs, herbs and potions. And he considered me in all my human glory, while the fresh handprint on my cheek tingled as I flushed under his scrutiny. He saw what had become of himself—and he accepted it with a single nod. "But many things have come to pass lately that have never happened before. Besides, I can't think of anyone who'd dare challenge the word of Droko...the Mystic."

26

SILVER

"Oh spider dear, with legs so long
Webs so pretty, silk so strong
You'll be a wonder to behold
In the menagerie, so bold
Our journey's long, but worry not
We'll dance and sing, and have a lot
Of fun and games, along the way—"

The cart stopped with a jolt and a shudder as Prancy plodded to a halt and planted her hooves. "What's this all about?" I asked her. "I thought you adored my impromptu ballads."

The donkey replied with an affronted splutter.

I hadn't chosen Prancy for her perky footwork—obviously—but she didn't usually give up on me so quickly. "What's wrong, did the mash those orcs fed you disagree with your delicate constitution? I'll have you know you ate the very same feed as their prize warhorse."

Prancy's ear swiveled. Not toward me...but toward the bushes.

That donkey might be as stubborn and slow as they came,

but her sense of self-preservation was just as highly developed as mine—a trait that should never be taken for granted.

My tooled leather bracers are certainly quite fetching, but they're not just for show. With a practiced flick of my wrist, I drew a throwing star sheathed in the fancywork into my palm. You don't normally see the weapons outside the desert. But the Blood Nomads had been amenable enough to make a trade once they sampled my supply of fine gnomish brandy.

The sharp baubles were not only well-made and nice to look at—but deceptively lethal.

Just like me.

Whoever was creeping up on me was stealthy, I'd give them that. I still didn't hear them myself, though Prancy's expressive eyes told me everything I needed to know. I readied the bladed star with a steadying breath, but went on chitchatting as if I hadn't a care in the world.

"Don't play lame with me, missie. That tease of a groom looked you over and said you were fit enough, so—"

I whirled around just as the figure cleared the undergrowth—and immediately threw his gangly arms over his head in surrender. "Come now, Silver. Is that any way to greet a friend?"

Crespash? "Hah, lucky for you I half-expected the red-headed boy to come track me down. Otherwise, your jugular would be gushing like a tapped keg."

"Lucky, huh?" The goblin made a dismissive gesture with the stumps of his stolen fingertips. "I wouldn't go *that* far. But if there's room at your camp, I'll share the watch."

He didn't need to keep watch. A goblin could squeeze into anything from a gap in the rocks to a fallen log, and any potential predators would be none the wiser. What he really wanted to share was my meal. But since I had an abundance of smoked orcish eel to spare—and since he was a more entertaining conversationalist than Prancy—I beckoned for him to join me.

Not too close, though.

I may be friendly—but I'm no idiot.

I saw to building the campfire, stacking dry branches in a careful pyramid while Crespash sprawled against a tree, scratching his armpit with a twig. He couldn't have been less help if he'd tried, but at least he'd brought news.

"As for the human, you won't be seeing him anytime soon. He's too smitten with my former master to even consider leaving Droko's side."

Former master? Interesting. "I suppose love makes fools of us all." I scraped some kindling together and struck my flint. Nothing. Again. Still nothing. "Though how any man could choose chains over freedom is beyond me."

"I'd certainly never trust myself to the tender mercies of an orc...then again, I've never seen one as besotted as Droko. Who knows? Maybe the two of them *will* live happily ever after."

"And if you believe that bedtime story, I'll sell you a map to the lost treasure of the Hill Giants, cheap." The spark finally caught. The dry plant fluff crackled, flame licking up the twigs. "Well anyway, here's to unlikely—"

Crespash lunged forward, emptying his waterskin over my carefully built fire. My hand flew to my throwing star, but he didn't attack me in the darkness. Instead, he pressed a finger to his lips and beckoned.

Curious, I followed him through the brush to the edge of a nearby clearing. The moonlight revealed what he'd heard—dozens of orcs in the distance moving through the trees. A raid heading for the village I'd just left? Supposedly, there was a truce between Red Hand and Two Swords—or so each side of the river claimed. But on closer inspection, I saw these weren't the proud Two Swords warriors who always bought up my finest whetstones. This was a ragged bunch, plodding along in no particular hurry.

Clearly, they'd be in need of some provisions....

As I rose to fetch my cart, the goblin caught me by the sleeve, hissing as the silk slipped through his absent claws. "Where d'you think you're going?" he spat.

"Off to ply my social graces. And a few of my wares."

"Then you're even dumber than you look! That's not just any old gaggle of orcs—that's the Lost Clan."

Never had the pleasure. Carefully, I drew out my brass far-seeker, a clever bit of gnomish craft that had paid for itself a hundred times over, and put the tiny cylinder to my eye to take stock of the group. Mostly men. A few women. No young. Their armor was piecemeal, held together with crude repairs. Many carried clubs, not swords. And some had no weapons at all.

"They hardly look like a threat," I said.

"The Lost Clan drifts between territories, demanding food and shelter wherever they go. No orc would dream of turning them away—bad luck, you see."

I watched as several more ragged orcs emerged from the trees. "Surely they'd appreciate my selection of—"

"You're not hearing me, peddler. They don't buy." Crespash's voice dropped even lower. "They take."

A crude wagon drawn by a pair of weary orcs brought up the rear. It creaked to a halt. From the back, they hauled down a massive wooden chest, its iron bands gleaming dully in the moonlight. Through the crowd, one particular orc moved like water through stones—never pushing, yet somehow always finding space. His armor was as shabby as the others, but he wore those patches like a king's cloak. With a practiced ease that caught my merchant's eye, he lifted the heavy lid as if it weighed nothing, revealing the treasure within.

I expected the usual plunder, spices and silver, baubles and gold. Instead, something far more interesting emerged: a figure unfurling from the confined space with the fluid grace of spilled ink.

It was a man—a human man—with midnight hair that fell past his shoulders in a wild tangle. Between his knife-edge cheekbones and those watchful dark eyes, he had the look of someone who'd seen far too much. Intricate tattoos covered his chest and arms—spiraling designs that seemed to shift in the moonlight, telling stories I couldn't quite read. Despite the cold, a simple loincloth was his only covering, revealing more of those cunning patterns wending down his body.

I twisted the lens on my far-seeker to get a better look.

"Still eager to trade with them?" Crespash muttered. "That poor sap could just as easily be you."

Most of the orcs ignored the tattooed human and went about setting up a crude camp. But while the ragged leader looked on with calculated satisfaction, a few of the others started toying with their captive. They circled him, jeering and prodding. But his eyes went flat and his expression utterly blank.

Can't break what you can't reach.

One particularly big and filthy orc traced the markings

on the human's chest with the tip of his eating knife—not cutting, just threatening—while others made sport of guessing the tattoos' meanings. Their prisoner stood still as stone, though his hand trembled ever so slightly.

Crespash shot me a sidelong glance. "Gonna play hero?"

I tucked away my scope and smiled thinly. "You've clearly mistaken me for a fighter, my friend, when I am but a lowly costermonger. I may be bold—but I have no death wish. Besides, if anything happened to me, who would look after my fine spider?"

"The spider you'll sell to the highest bidder."

"Indeed I will. Though I confess, part of me wishes I could linger to watch tomorrow's entertainment." I gathered Prancy's reins and nodded toward the road ahead. "What say we find a campsite well away from here? A wise merchant knows when the market's about to turn...deadly."